Brightest Dawn

Book Three of the
What She Knew Trilogy

K. R. Hughes
T. L. Burns

Master Koda Select Publishing

Disclaimer

Working on this trilogy was both fun and educational, though it is purely fictional. We scoured the local library and internet for any and all resources from the time period and then together, we weaved our own theory about what could have happened on that dark day in 1963 and the ensuing months. As with all good fictional stories, we leave it to you the reader to determine how much could be true, but more importantly, to enjoy the what if . . .

This is a work of historical fiction. All names, characters, and incidents are used fictitiously.

Connect with us on our website at:

www.whatsheknew.wix.com/kandtproductions

Preface

As we began the final book of this trilogy, we struggled with how to end the incredible journey we had taken Marilyn and the rest of the gang on. After all the entire trilogy is about Marilyn and her unlived life. We had to decide on how she would have wanted to spend her remaining time on earth. With that in mind, we chose to take her down the twisting turning path we'd set before her and then give her the world she'd always longed for.

Recap: **Fateful Night**, book one in the **What She Knew** trilogy opens in late July 1962, just before the night of Marilyn's 'suicide' and ends with President John F. Kennedy's motorcade on Nov 22, 1963 in Dealey Plaza.

Recap: **Darkest Day**, the second book in the **What She Knew** trilogy picks up where book one leaves off. Did Kennedy die on that darkest of days or was there some mystery involved? On Nov 22, 1963, Kennedy isn't on a world tour, but in the Alps recovering from back surgery, something no one knew about, not even Jacquelyn Kennedy.

As the dark forces of the world are trying to start a nuclear war with America, Robert Kennedy runs interference. He has to keep Jack Kennedy's secret as well as find a peaceful solution to all of the enemies who were trying to invade the United States. Can our unlikely gang of heroes save our nation from ruin? Find out in this, the final book of our trilogy.

Special Thanks

Jodi Thomas has been instrumental in the creative process for this trilogy. Without her influence, these three novels, as well as the imagination it took to create them would not have been possible. Ms. Thomas is an amazing mentor, as well as one of the kindest most encouraging souls on this planet. Thank you! Thank you for your belief, support, and cheerleading sessions. We truly appreciate you.

Chapter 1

<u>August 4, 1964</u>

Barbara Hadley stood opened mouthed staring at the taillights of the van rushing out of sight. Two black sedans, with agents in them, sped past her through the parking area to try to catch the van. Moving out of the middle of the street, Barbara screamed, "Oh no! Where are they taking Marilyn? I mean Norma?"

"Ms. Hadley?" An agent had reached her, "Are you all right?"

Dazed, Barbara looked into the face of a tall seasoned agent and nodded her head "Yes, but they took Norma. I nursed her back to health, I'm her best friend, and I don't know what to do. What if they kill her?"

He gently took her arm and led her toward his own vehicle. He opened the car door for her, and then motioned for her to sit.

She sat down, leaving her feet firmly on the pavement as sirens filled the air along with the blaring lights of several cop cars and an ambulance.

"I'm Agent Gregory Morris. I need to ask you a few questions." He smiled warmly and Barbara blushed.

Thank God it's dark and he can't see me blush. Barbara shook herself mentally before she nodded. *Sorry Norma, but he's a hunk.*

Jack Lancer touched the swollen lips of Mary Meyer, his longtime lover, in a slow lingering kiss before he rolled off of her. She snuggled into the safety of his arms as he drew the sheet up over their naked bodies.

"It's so nice to have you here as Jack Lancer, a nobody, as opposed to always trying to eke-out some time alone when you were John F. Kennedy, President of the United States. I much prefer having you all to myself."

"I do too," he stroked her hair with one hand.

"You've improved in your skills, Jack. I don't know what happened to you in the past two years, but you've gotten better since you came back from the Alps." Mary kissed his forearm as she tucked the sheet under her arm.

"Well the nurses in Switzerland were most helpful in explaining about the joys of great love making. As Greta was quick to point out, I had the mind of a world leader as the President of the U.S., why did I have the most unsatisfactory manners in bed?" He kissed her temple and stroked her silky hair.

"I think you should thank her from me." Mary laughed.

"Oh, I already thanked her." Jack snorted then started to sit up.

"Don't go."

"I'll be right back. I just need to work out the kinks in my back. You should consider joining an acrobatic team, my dear. You've got the flexibility for it." Jack leaned over to kiss her once more, tousling her hair with deft fingers before standing up.

She watched him while he did some stretches, unaware that the sheet had slipped down to her waist while she propped herself up against the pillows for a better view.

Papa Doc Duvalier, President of Haiti, stomped off the pier after Aristotle Onassis had left. His advisers met him at the end of the dock. "That smug son of a bitch thinks he's going to get that Kennedy woman to marry him and bring him into the precious circle of the Americans. I need a curse for Onassis that will keep him from getting his damn shipping industry in their ports."

One of the advisors nodded and peeled off from the group. "I know that blonde bimbo is alive and I'll prove it if it's the last thing I do. No one makes a fool out of me."

The smoke filled the helicopter as the gas fumes nearly choked everyone on board. Agent Bill Walton struggled with one of the henchmen while Norma Baker gave a mighty kick, sending her attacker out of the helicopter, screaming to his death on the jagged rocks below.

Norma jumped back as the helicopter took a hard turn nearly forcing her out of the open door. She screamed as she grabbed a hold of the seat behind her and pulled herself back to safety. Struggling to stand upright she made her way to the injured pilot who was battling to keep the spinning copter from crashing into the side of the Canadian mountain.

Bill managed to get behind the man he was fighting with and gave his head a sickening twist, breaking his neck with practiced ease. He dropped the body and rushed to Norma's side. Bill took the pilot's neck and forced him to steer close to the mountain.

"Land here." Bill demanded.

Bobby Kennedy watched Ethel as she poured the freshly brewed cup of coffee for her husband. She placed a couple of chocolate chip cookies on a small plate and turned toward the kitchen table.

"This is by far the best part of the day. I wait for it." Ethel handed him the coffee and sat down across from him. She placed the cookies between them as he took her free hand.

"Me too. It's what gives me a sense of sanity in this maddening world. Did you hear what Lyndon Johnson is up to now? He's sending more troops over to Vietnam. I can't believe him. What is he thinking?"

Ethel opened her mouth to answer but he rushed on. "Did you know that Howard Hunt is a double agent? He's the one who's keeping Fidel Castro alive! So now the CIA hates us more than ever."

"Who?" Ethel managed to get a word in.

"Us. The Kennedys. Me especially." Bobby ran his fingers through his hair and sipped some black coffee.

"Honey, you should really just give up trying to convince Johnson that you want to be his running mate. It's making you crazy. You don't agree with anything he does." Ethel stood up and walked behind her husband's chair to massage his shoulders and neck.

He reached up and grabbed hold of her hands, "You know I can't do that. I owe it to Jack and the country needs someone who's not a raving lunatic in office. You know I'd rather shoot LBJ myself than be his damn running mate but I have to try."

"I know."

Bobby finished his coffee and started to put on his jacket. "I have to go. I'll be home later. Don't wait up." He planted a kiss on her forehead and left. Ethel stood in the kitchen shaking her head.

Papa Doc stormed up and down the wide hallway of his mansion waiting with increasing impatience for his "guests" to be escorted to their rooms. He swung wide to turn back in the opposite direction, knocking an unsuspecting maid into the potted fern she was watering.

She started to say something but closed her mouth tight, and sat in the fern until Papa Doc had marched away. She got up with the stealth of a sniper, dusted herself off, and crept back toward the servants' quarters.

"What are we going to do?" Mary wondered as she moved toward the nightstand for a cigarette.

Jack continued to exercise for a moment before he looked at her, a serious expression on his face. "I can't ever go back. I'm Jack Lancer now and I need to make a new life."

"I understand that," she huffed. "I meant specifically. What are we going to do?"

"It has occurred to me that I could just live here while you worked and spied for me. I still don't really know which of my enemies would go so far as to actually shoot me."

Mary shook her head, "You can't live here. I'm sure I'm being watched. Followed. I'm not a safe haven for you, Jack."

He returned to the bed, took her unlit cigarette, and tossed it to the night stand, then gathered her into his arms. "I'll protect you. I'll tell Bobby to find out who's bothering you and call them off. Don't worry, Mary. I still have a few friends."

Lady Bird Johnson, the First Lady of the United States, waited until the cameras and news crews cleared the Oval Office. Lyndon was sitting back in his chair smoking a cigarette and relaxing for the moment with his feet on the desk. She allowed him a few minutes while she relived his speech.

"The determination of all Americans to carry out our full commitment to the people and to the government of South Vietnam will be redoubled by this outrage. Yet our response, for the present, will be limited and fitting. We Americans know, although others appear to forget, the risks of spreading conflict. We still seek no wider war."

She smiled at the brave words, "Lyndon, I repeat my question. Why did you tell the Soviets we didn't want to pursue war after Hanoi?"

The President sat up and put his feet on the floor, "Because after the Tonkin incident, we don't need to stir up more trouble in the world."

"But you want war in Vietnam. It would mean a great deal of money for us in the munitions industry."

"Yes, my dear, but the public doesn't need to know that, nor does the world." Lyndon stood up and came around the desk. He kissed the top of her head and walked out.

"No, don't get Bobby involved. I'll talk to Cord. He may be able to help me. Even though he's my ex, we're still close." Mary begged as Jack gripped her arm.

"I won't have that scum bag helping you or anybody. He's the worst kind of man there is." He gripped her harder, "Your ex-husband is known for the dirty way he gets things done in the CIA. I don't think we should trust anyone. Everyone is a bad guy and nobody is what they seem." Jack rubbed a hand through his hair and looked like a lost little boy for a moment.

"You've changed." She pulled free of his embrace. "You're no longer the confident, good looking hero. You're lost and alone like the rest of the world." Mary shook her head as sadness enveloped her.

"What did you expect? Jackie won't have me back. I have nowhere to go and no way to make anything of my life. That would change anyone. I should be dead. It would be much better if I were."

Mary smacked him hard on the shoulder. "Don't say that! I need you."

"I'm glad someone does." He placed his arms around her, pulling her closer to him, and kissed the top of her head. "Who do you think is following you?"

"I don't know, but they've been here." She leaned away from his embrace and shivered a little. "They've looked through my things and its creepy knowing they've rifled through my stuff, but I'm sure they want the diary."

"Why didn't you destroy it?" he pushed a stray hair behind her ear, giving her a concerned look.

"It has a lot of great secrets and my sketches in it and I want to keep them fresh in my mind."

"Secrets?" He sat straight up, pulling her with him onto his lap, crushing her with his intensity. "What secrets do you wish to keep, Mary?"

"The repeated attempts of the CIA trying to have Castro assassinated for one."

Chapter 2

Castro waited for Sam Giancana, one of the lead mafia bosses from the United States, to cross the expansive lawn so they could speak in private. Sam came to a stop next to Castro's massive lawn chair and parked himself in the somewhat smaller one set up across from the dictator.

"It looks like there's no getting through to Khrushchev. Get him out."

Giancana nodded and stood up. "I'll take care of it."

Bobby sat watching TV in the den waiting to hear that Norma was safe and that his concern had been for nothing. He pretended interest in the program when Ethel smiled or laughed at something the host said. *Damn it! Why haven't I gotten a call?*

The pilot struggled to get the copter settled on a plateau. Once they were on the ground Bill performed the same neck breaking maneuver on the pilot and shut down the engine.

9

Grabbing Norma by the hand he dragged her from the wreckage.

"Wait, I'm missing a shoe. I can't possibly climb down without it." Norma gestured to her bare foot.

Bill climbed back up into the copter and returned with a couple of coats, a pair of combat boots and what looked like an emergency kit. He handed her the boots and waited while she quickly put them on.

He laughed at the comically big boots on her petite feet. "Sorry, it's the best we can do for now."

She grinned, "My hero!"

Bill turned back to the helicopter, hurriedly cut the fuel line, and lit a match.

He grabbed Norma's hand as the front passenger seat began to blaze. "Let's get out of here. It might blow up."

"Why did you do that?" Norma looked confused as she ran beside Bill in the floppy boots.

"I wanted to send a signal to whoever may be following us that the crash was deadly. Hopefully they'll think it was their own men who lived and we died in the wreckage."

"*My hero!*" Norma exaggerated the words for a second time in five minutes.

J Edgar Hoover, director of the F.B.I., sat at his desk late into the evening staring at the reports regarding the power grab President Johnson was making. He tapped the pencil against the folder and pinched his nose with his thumb and forefinger. The headache that had been threatening broke through as he slammed the folder shut and threw the pencil across the room. "Damn it! I guess I'll need to talk to Robert Kennedy about this mess. Maybe he'll know what's going on since he's the Attorney General."

Agent Gregory Morris finished up with Barbara, "Thank you Ms. Hadley. Here is my number if you have any questions or can think of anything else. Since we have the man who struck you in custody, you can expect to be hearing from us about pressing charges."

"I do want to press charges and I do want to know where Miss Baker is. You boys better find her quick before she gets killed."

"Don't worry, Ms. Hadley, she has Agent Walton with her. He jumped in the van and they took him as well. She is safe. No doubt." Agent Morris assured her.

"Well, I don't know how he can protect her if they kill him first," Ms. Hadley huffed.

"He's a good man, so don't you worry. We'll call you as soon as we hear anything. Try to get some rest." He patted her shoulder and walked away.

"Mr. Kennedy, we have one of them in custody." Agent Wes Latimer was trying to reassure Bobby over the phone.

"But you don't have Norma, and we've lost sight of the van. Has our suspect said anything relevant?"

"Not yet. He's refusing to talk at all. Apparently Morris upset him when he first brought him in. The suspect won't even tell us his name."

"Well, withhold food, drink, and bathroom privileges. That'll make him talk. If not, try something more convincing, Latimer. We need to know where they are."

"Walton has a good head on his shoulders. I believe he'll do everything in his power to get them free."

"I do too, Latimer. Keep me posted on this situation." Bobby hung up the phone as Ethel placed her arms around his neck. He let out a long sigh and burrowed his nose into her hair. "They got Norma and Walton. Holy shit!"

"They'll find them. Don't worry. You've got the best agents anywhere tailing them. She'll come back safe." Ethel massaged his shoulders as she spoke.

"They better or I'll have the lot of them stand before a firing squad."

Jackie Kennedy blew a smoke ring at her sister. "Really Lee, why do you always think I've done something?"

"Usually, because you have." Lee watched for a moment before her attention was drawn to her niece and nephew laughing on the lawn.

"You wouldn't understand if I told you. Besides it isn't my fault."

"What?" Lee smiled and waved at Caroline as she chased the ball John-John had kicked.

"It wasn't my fault and I'm not taking the blame." Jackie remained oddly defiant.

"Fine. No blame. What happened?" Lee stubbed out the cigarette in the ashtray. She picked up her iced tea from the table between their chairs.

"I think Papa Doc drugged me with some type of truth serum."

Lee spewed the sip of tea into the air. "Oh dear, you've been reading too many spy novels. Or have you been seeing a secret agent?" Lee laughed for a moment, but caught the frown on her sister's face. "Okay, I'm sorry. Tell me when this happened."

"At the coffee shop a few days or maybe a week ago, I don't really remember. I do recall thinking I had seen Jack. He was walking outside the coffee shop looking in and then he turned and walked away with his head hung."

"Jackie, darling, you're not making sense. Did you go see someone about your grief?"

"It really happened. I've told you he's alive. Why won't you believe me?" Jackie stood up and stormed into the house.

Aristotle Onassis leaned forward to help Zsa-Zsa Gabor onto the Christina, "Welcome ladies! It's a pleasure to have two such Hollywood Divas take time out to go for a ride on my yacht."

Zsa-Zsa grasped his hand and pulled herself up, allowing her breast to brush against his arm as she climbed the short ladder. He grinned and pulled her up by the waist. He kissed her full on the lips and released her. Zsa-Zsa pouted as she walked over to the waiter holding a tray full of champagne.

Ava followed her sister, but boldly kissed Ari as she was hoisted onboard the yacht. "Ari, dah-lin' it's good to see you."

Onassis grinned down at her as he took one hand and ran it over her bikini clad bottom. "Fabulous as usual, Ava. Come on and we'll get this party going."

The engine roared to life and they began to glide out toward the open water. The trio stepped onto the deck. Ava quickly covered her startled gasp and smiled at the man sitting on a deck chair.

"Sam. What a surprise to see you!" Ava covered the space between them and leaned down to kiss the air above his cheek.

Sam stared at her breasts struggling to stay inside the string bikini top until she stood up and he had an eye level gaze at her navel. "You're looking well, Ava."

"But of course, dah-lin'. I must retain my figure for the fans."

"Naturally." Ari gave her an approving pat on her bottom as he lifted a fresh champagne glass off of a tray. He lifted the glass to his lips, keeping his eyes on hers while he sipped it. "Relax, sit down, and have fun."

Ava and Zsa-Zsa exchanged glances and sat down on the same lounge chair. Ava grabbed a beach towel off the chair and wrapped it around her suddenly chilled body, even though the sun blazed down on her skin.

Agent Rex Stansel drummed his fingers on Bobby's desk with impatience as he waited for Bobby to show up. He nearly jumped out of the cushy chair when Bobby abruptly appeared from behind a wall.

Bobby smiled as he leaned across the desk and shook Stansel's hand. "Spill."

Stansel cleared his throat and picked up the notebook he had laid on the desk, "Suspects were chased into Virginia by me and several other agents including the local police. We pulled into an open field just moments behind the van, but it was empty. I realized that there was a helicopter getting ready to take off and opened fire as I ran toward them. The other officers and agents followed suit."

Bobby interrupted at this point, "Shit! Are you trying to tell me they got away from you fucking idiots?"

Stansel grimaced and returned to his notes, "The unmarked helicopter did escape without incident. We were afraid that our victims would be injured if we succeeded in bringing the copter down."

Bobby steepled his fingers and nodded for Stansel to continue. "Point taken."

Stansel looked at Bobby, "We did a thorough investigation of the van. We found there had been a struggle. Apparently someone is injured because there was a lot of blood. We believe Agent Walton was the one who did the damage."

"Anything else?"

"Yes. There was a shoe found in the back of the van. It was the one with the transponder."

"Holy Mother of God!"

"You know Walton will protect her even though we no longer have any way of tracking them."

"You better hope he does." Bobby stood up and stormed back through the tiny opening in the wall.

Sam Giancana approached Ari as he sat surrounded by the usual array of beautiful Greek women. He sat down across from Onassis, grabbed a drink and a cigar.

"Something on your mind?" Onassis watched as Sam puffed to get the cigar lit.

"Kennedy." Sam continued to work on the cigar until the soft glow began at the tip.

"Ladies, you'll excuse me for a moment?" Ari shoved the gorgeous lady from his lap.

She pouted, but followed the others to the upper deck.

"There's a lot of talk going on about the Kennedys. Which one and what is the problem?" Onassis sipped his drink.

"It seems everyone is gunning for the death of all Kennedys. I realize that the Edward Kennedy accident was probably just that, an accident, but in my circles there is talk. There is also speculation as to why the Kennedys in particular would be so widely hated." Sam watched Ari's face; the man betrayed no emotion.

"Because they are America's favorite politicians and they have too much sway in public thinking."

"They're not as powerful as you think. Now that Joe is mostly out of the picture, the others are trying to clean up organized crime. The word is that Robert Kennedy has joined forces with J. Edgar Hoover in the crusade to stop organized crime and the way we've always run things."

"So?" Onassis sat up and refilled his drink from the decanter at his elbow.

"So, we need to lay off. The only way you'll win this little war is by playing nice. The death of another

Kennedy will not sit well with the Americans. They already suspect you of dirty dealings and they don't like you. Perhaps, if you want to win this one, you'll change tactics."

"Who the hell do you think you are to tell me what to do or how to run my business?" Onassis yelled.

"Just some friendly advice. You do pay me to find out the latest dirt on everything. Just doing my job." Sam got up and left Ari fuming.

Chapter 3

August 7, 1964

Bill Walton sat watching the trap he'd built out of twigs to entrap a small animal. Norma leaned against a rock watching in silence. Bill noticed a white rabbit sniffing around the trap. He waited until the bunny hopped into the confines of the trap and pulled the string to make the trap collapse trapping the bunny inside.

Norma jumped up and yelled, "Yes! You got him!!"

Bill smiled as he replaced his shoe lace and got the bunny out of the trap. "You know I have to kill it now."

"I can't watch. I've got to do something else. Poor little thing." Norma leaned down to the terrified rabbit.

"He's dinner, so don't get too attached." Bill waited until she was gone before he quickly broke the neck and began skinning it.

Kenny O'Donnell, aide to the President, sat at his desk in front of the Oval Office working when his phone rang. He picked it up with impatience. "O'Donnell."

"Kenny, I need a mole in the Onassis home in New York. The kids are there, so work out a tutor or teacher, or something." Bobby didn't wait for a response. He hung up, leaving a buzzing noise in Kenny's ear.

Lyndon Johnson watched the water swirl around in the fountain in the park across the street from the White House. He turned as a man approached him. "Clifford, I have a huge problem."

"Then you've called in the right man." Clark Clifford, confidante to the President, lit a cigarette and watched the normally poised Johnson tremble a little.

"Robert Kennedy."

"Yes, I know of him." Clark smirked.

Johnson shot him a go-to-hell look and continued. "Kennedy has it in his mind to advance in politics. He wants to be on the ticket as my running mate. There are many reasons why that won't work. He needs to be persuaded to reconsider."

"That sounds like a job for an office flunky. What do you need me for?"

"I want him eliminated." Johnson walked away leaving Clark staring after him.

Ethel listened to the phone ring on the other end of the receiver for five rings before Pat Kennedy Lawford picked it up.

"Hello?" Pat sounded sleepy.

"Oh, I hope I didn't wake you. I was just calling to see how you're doing." Ethel twisted the phone cord around her fingers idly while she spoke.

"It's fine. I was just dozing a little bit. I'm doing okay. You know, as well as can be expected."

"Have you heard from Peter?" Ethel hated to ask her sister-in-law, but she was dying for information.

"Not since we decided to separate. We're looking into a potential divorce, but we're still trying to figure it out."

"I'm so sorry. Please know I'm here if you need anything." Ethel leaned forward, preparing to hang up.

"I guess Daddy was right. He's a playboy and I fell for that 'I'll be faithful and true to you' routine he seems so fond of giving everyone." Pat sniffed.

"Men can be such rats. Do you want me to sic the secret service on him? Follow him, to make him paranoid?" Ethel joked, but it was lost on Pat.

"No, don't waste government resources like that."

"Jackie?"

Jacqueline nearly jumped out of her skin. She had been deep in thought staring out the window and hadn't heard Bobby approaching her.

"You nearly scared me to death." Jackie leaned into his embrace and hugged him for a moment. He laughed softly and let her go.

"I'm sorry."

"What are you doing here?"

Bobby plopped himself into a chair in the spacious living area and motioned for her to do the same.

"Would you like a coke or some coffee?"

He shook his head and ran his fingers through his hair in much the same manner that John had done.

"I can't stay long. I just needed to ask you something."

Jackie took a seat opposite him while he grasped her hands in his.

"This seems serious. You're quite intense." Jackie squeezed his hands gently leaving them clasped in his.

"Do you remember the aftermath of John's death and how we both suspected who might have done it?"

"Johnson. Yes, I do remember that, but nothing ever came of it." Jackie pulled her hands free and fidgeted in her chair. "You know this topic causes me distress."

"I know and I'm sorry to bring it up but there has been a new threat on my life and it reeked of the types of threats John received just before . . . ."

"Oh no, Bobby! Are you really so concerned that you have come to me for reassurance? This is awful." Jackie jumped up from her chair and paced the room.

"Yes, it is horrible. I think Johnson wants me killed. He doesn't want me to be on the political ticket and he will do whatever it takes to keep me from advancing my agenda."

"Is being a Vice President so important to you? Just wait and run in four years." Jackie stopped pacing to stare at him, "I don't know why you need to be in the oval office at all. Politics have brought nothing good into this family."

"Because, Jackie darling girl, we need to change the world. Right the wrongs and help those less fortunate. I can do that."

Castro listened to Nikita Khrushchev, Premier of the Soviet Union, on the other end of the crackling phone line. "So you gave away our nuclear advantage? So you're now in bed with the Americans?" Castro blew a smoke ring from his cigar.

He listened for another moment, "Well if that's your position, I'll just take my interests elsewhere or maybe find me a Soviet who will back me." Castro rang off with Khrushchev.

Lionel Grandison, coroner for Los Angeles, leaned over the corpse on the cold metal table and prepared to make the first incision for the autopsy. At twenty-four, he was still one of the youngest coroners in Los Angeles, and famous for the conclusion about sex goddess Marilyn Monroe's cause of death. He sighed at the memory and pushed the scalpel just under the collar bone of the deceased man.

The double doors to the morgue burst open, and a hulking man in a black mask ran toward him. Grandison used the scalpel in his hand to slash at his assailant. The two men struggled as the scalpel dropped onto the floor. The huge man struck Grandison across the face with the back of his hand and then sucker punched him in the gut. Lionel landed backward on the corpse and quickly ducked under the table to the other side.

The masked man laughed as he pushed the table against Lionel until he was firmly backed into the corner.

"What do you want?" Lionel's voice was barely heard in the suddenly silent cold room.

"Come with me." The masked man grabbed him by the collar of the shirt and shoved the table away roughly, knocking the corpse onto the floor with a heavy thud.

"Why?" Lionel struggled against the big man, but was clearly over-powered. "Who are you?"

The masked man continued to push Lionel forward without an answer.

"Answer me you coward!"

The man stopped as he pulled Grandison up to his tiptoes, "Shut. The. Hell. Up."

Lionel nodded and allowed himself to be swept out the door into the warm starry night.

Walter Jenkins, military aide and confidante of Johnson's, sat in the limo awaiting the President. Johnson slid into the seat beside Jenkins and the driver moved into traffic.

"What's going on with those gunships?" Johnson asked. "I want them ready to fly within a few weeks."

"We're making progress," Jenkins shifted to look at Lyndon, "as you know they are being re-welded to allow side shooting. We've got about a dozen that'll be ready to go in a few days."

"I'm glad the Pentagon went for the refitting of the old World War II planes. This saves our government some money and allows us to have troops in the air and on the ground. After the Gulf of Tonkin Resolution, I get to have as much fire power as I want." Johnson nearly clapped his hands with glee.

"We both know that was a made up attack." Jenkins shook his head, "Nevertheless it has been a huge boon to my pocket book."

The limo slowed to a stop, and Jenkins opened the door, "Have a nice war, Lyndon."

"Thanks to Puff the Magic Dragon, we sure will." Johnson leaned back as Jenkins shut the door and the limo went back to the White House. *What a great name for gunships.*

Norma leaned against a tree, exhausted and hungry. She'd been so busy concentrating on where she was walking and keeping the stupid boots on her feet that she had barely said two words to Bill. *Bill is so good at catching dinner and building fires. I can't believe how great his survival skills are.*

She smiled as she heard the gentle snore coming from the dying campfire. *It'll be getting cold soon and I'll need to cuddle up with him, but not yet.*

Norma twisted some long pieces of dead grass together as she tried to wrangle her thoughts. *Barbara asked me what I was going to do with my life. What am I going to do with it?*

She rubbed the back of her neck, picked up her boots, and crept over to Bill. They had snuggled up for the warmth for the last two nights. It was cold at night, but warm enough during the day. She moved a twig as she positioned herself into his strong arms. He sighed and pulled her closer.

*Truly, what **am** I going to do?* She settled her head against his forearm and closed her eyes, *I'm not good at anything normal.* Exhaustion over took her and she settled into a restless slumber.

Papa Doc Duvalier stormed across the grand hall into the massive library, startling the man who had been starring out across the raging sea. It was stormy and Papa Doc's countenance matched the weather. The presidential palace was usually filled with ruckus, but this afternoon it was eerily quiet.

"It's about time you showed up with a report." Duvalier growled as he lit a cigar and blew the smoke into the face of Felipe Barbot.

"I haven't had much to tell you. Kennedy didn't show up at the meeting place. The helicopter took off on schedule, but there has been no word from the pilot since."

Papa Doc's fury turned his face puce, "What the bloody hell do you mean? Where are they? Felipe, give me the answer I'm looking for."

"The copter didn't land on the island at the appointed time." His reply was barely audible. "We've had a man searching the perimeter for two days now with no sign of them."

"Them? The pilot and who else?"

"Our two men and a man and the woman." Felipe's voice was a bit stronger.

"Five? That's a full load. What man?" Papa Doc tapped cigar ash on to Barbot's hand. He flinched but didn't move as terror crept into his heart.

"We don't know."

Ava had begun to relax after several drinks. She watched Ari with weariness. He continued to talk to Sam in low whispered tones as he ignored the women. She glanced over at Zsa-Zsa who had dozed off.

Ari turned to her so abruptly that she nearly choked on the champagne. "So Ava, tell me what you've been doing with yourself." Ari moved closer to her and sat on a deck chair brushing his hand across her bare knee.

"I've been taking a little break dah-lin."

"Good. Good. Everyone needs a vacation." Ari stroked her thigh and she jumped at the touch. "My dear, why are you so nervous? When I told you that you were off the hook for the tapes I meant it. I'm a man of my word."

Ava visibly relaxed, "Of course you are, dah-lin."

The smack across her beautiful face was so sudden and forceful she fell off the chair as she wiped blood from the side of her mouth. As she looked up into his hard eyes, he held out a hand to help her up. "Now we're paid in full."

Stansel entered the room where the assailant was sitting on the uncomfortable folding chair. He handed the man a cup of coffee and sat down across the table from him. "I can help you if you'll let me."

The man glared at him without answer. He picked up the cup of coffee and turned the glass upside down spilling the hot contents all over the table. Stansel shoved his chair back to avoid the steamy liquid.

"Have it your way then. We can and will keep you until we figure this out."

Bobby Kennedy answered the buzzer, "What is it?" he shifted the papers on his desk.

"J. Edgar Hoover is on the line for you, sir."

"Put the call through." Bobby sighed. *What does he want?*

"Kennedy?" Hoover bellowed into the phone. "We need to have a face to face. I've got some information for you."

"I don't have time for this J. Edgar." Bobby leaned back in his chair.

"Oh, I think you do. I have information about a certain helicopter that took off in Virginia, the very same one that your agents failed to take down."

"I can meet you in an hour." Bobby carefully put the receiver back in the cradle.

Chapter 4

Jack paced around Kenny's place. He was restless and bored. He picked up the phone to call Jackie, decided against it and replaced the receiver. *Damn, I can't call her. She'll just hang up. I miss my kids, my life, hell my whole clan. I should have just died. This is no way to spend a life.* He sat down at the kitchen table and sobbed like a baby.

Ava watched Ari stand up and head toward the other guests. She quickly put on her wrap and tied it around her slim waist. Glancing around, she saw Frank Sinatra, singer and actor, lounging on the lower deck. She slipped on her pink heels and clicked her way down the stairs to him.

Frank smiled as he motioned to the waiter for a new round of drinks. He held up his hand and put up two fingers. "What can I do for you, Ava?"

Ava shrugged off her cover up and revealed a bikini underneath. She felt more confident when he was focused on her breasts instead of her face. "I need to get to Robert Kennedy."

Mary Meyer slunk into the back room of the beauty salon. Ethel peeked out from under a hair dryer and waved her over. The beautician brought over a tray filled with facial creams and beauty potions. She motioned the women to follow her.

Mary didn't say a word as Ethel stood up with a perfectly manicured hair style, grinned, and fell into step behind the other two women. "Thank you, Myrtle." Ethel said loud enough for the other women to notice her.

Once they were in a private room and seated on the comfy chairs, the beautician discretely left them alone.

Ethel leaned close to Mary, "Have you spoken to Cord yet?"

"No, he's been so busy. I've got an appointment to see him later tonight." Mary fidgeted with a loose thread on the chair.

"I hope he can help you. I know you've got to be terrified." Ethel patted Mary's arm. "You poor dear, I don't know how you've been so brave. I do wish Jack were here, he'd know what to do."

Mary looked up into the concerned face of her new friend and made the decision. "Ethel, I have to tell you something. John is alive."

"Jack?" Ethel's voice crackled on the single word. "You mean John Kennedy is still alive?"

Fidel Castro smiled at the flunky standing before him and offered him one of his famous Cuban cigars. The man eagerly took one and bit off the end as Castro held out a lighter to him.

Jose Fuegos smiled in appreciation, "What can I do for you?"

"I want that traitorous bitch, Marita. It'll be a difficult mission since she's being protected by the CIA.

But this is personal for me, and I know you won't fail me."

"You want her?"

"Dead."

"I'm telling you he is alive." Jackie insisted to her psycho-analyst.

"It is only natural that you miss him so much you believe you've seen him or heard him. It's a hallucination."

"No! He's alive." Jackie's tears formed at the corners of her eyes. "Why won't anyone believe me?"

"I don't wish to be crude, but we all have heard the accounts of how he was publicly shot and killed. You were there. You were on Air Force One guarding his casket and standing beside the new President, Lyndon Johnson. I'll give you a stronger prescription to help you overcome these delusions."

"They aren't delusions. He's alive. He's talked to me on the phone and I've seen him."

"Now Mrs. Kennedy, I'm sure you believe that with all of your heart. After all he was your husband and you must miss him terribly. Grief affects everyone in different ways."

"But I don't miss him. He won't leave me alone. He wants to be a family again. He wants to see the children." Jackie sat up and banged a slim hand on the desk.

"Perhaps it would be best if you moved somewhere away from this town where you won't have so many memories creeping around corners at you." The analyst took out his prescription pad, jotted down the information, then tore it off and handed it to her. "Our time is up for this week. Get these filled immediately and I'll see you next week."

"He's alive. You can go to Hell!" Jackie stormed out of the office with a determined fury.

"Why do you need to see Bobby?" Frank motioned for her to sit in the lounger beside him.

"I need a favor." Ava smiled as Frank raised his eyebrow.

"From me or Bobby?" Frank moved to light a cigarette.

Ava leaned in close and whispered, "Maybe both. Ari is after something Bobby has."

"What?" Frank smiled at her as Ari came nearer. Frank kissed the inside of her neck.

Ava played along, stroking his leg as she smooched at his ear, "The tapes. Ari wants them."

"Thank God it is summer or we'd freeze to death." Norma shivered in the over large coat as Bill struggled to make the kindling spark for the fire.

"I could warm you up." He grinned.

She tossed a pine cone at him.

"You know you want me too!" Bill protested as the pine cone hit him lightly on the leg. "Owwww! I'm wounded I need medical attention." He plopped himself down on the dirt, forgetting about the need for a fire.

"You can have 'medical attention' after you get that fire started. I'm cold and hungry." Norma smiled and threw him a wink.

"Oh you are naughty! I'm going to make sure I get my attention just as soon as I feed you." Bill blew in earnest on the kindling where a tiny flame was just sparking to life.

"I'm so glad you found that stream and we got us some trout."

"What are heroes supposed to do?" Bill added some logs to the fire and settled back against a rock.

"How long do you think it'll be before we get to civilization?" Norma scooted closer to him and he placed his arm around her shoulders, hugging her close to his side for warmth. *"Oh what I would give for a massage, hair dressing, and manicure. I really miss the limelight."*

"I'm hoping the Royal Canadian Mounties will find us soon."

"Is that code for 'I have no idea'?"

Lionel Grandison grunted as he was bodily removed from the back of a dark van by the masked man. He was shoved through a door and into a darkened room with a single light bulb, hanging from a string in the center of the room.

The masked man forced him onto a couch and stood to the side at attention. Another man entered the room and sat down on a chair across from the couch. Grandison merely watched the other man for a while until he spoke.

"What do you know about Marilyn Monroe's death?" The question broke the silence, startling Lionel out of his stupor.

"I know she's dead."

"Right."

Lionel watched the man for another minute before he offered, "She was murdered."

"I know that, but was it really Monroe?"

"Essentially, Johnson wants you to move out of his way." Hoover sat across from Bobby at a picnic table in a park. "He's getting upset that you won't let up on this vice president bid and I've heard that he wants to make you hush no matter how he needs to do it."

"I gathered. I've been receiving death threats that mimic those John got shortly before his assassination." Bobby sipped on a can of Tab.

"There were rumors Johnson was behind the hit, but we could not prove it. We need to do something to get him to slip up."

"I'm sure you'll come up with something, Hoover. I don't have the man power or the time, but I appreciate that you told me what he is up to. I'm thinking he's hired some goon to try to scare me."

"He's lost all grip on reality. He's never going to be elected if he doesn't have a strong running mate. You shouldn't be on the ticket." Hoover shook his head, "Perhaps we can come to an agreement to get Johnson away from this mad power grab he has going on."

"Agreed. What are you doing about Georgi Bolshakov, the Russian dual spy?" Bobby grimaced, "We still owe him for his help in the stand-off with the Soviets at Berlin's Checkpoint-Charlie in '61."

"Yes, he's still a valuable asset." Hoover took off his glasses and cleaned them on his handkerchief. He replaced them on his nose and uncrossed his legs. Hoover stood up and shook Bobby's hand. "By the way, that helicopter you've been looking for was found burned to a crisp in the Northern Canadian Mountains."

Mary smiled at Ethel's shock. "Yes, very much alive. I'm surprised Bobby hasn't told you."

"What? Bobby knew?" Ethel nearly shouted then clamped a hand over her mouth.

"The whole time. The poor man who was shot in Dealey Plaza was an impersonator filling in while Jack had back surgery in Switzerland."

"Robert Francis Kennedy you're in so much trouble! He is going to need protection from his wife!"

Mary's laugh sounded genuine. "Look, I'm sorry I had to tell you but John and I have been seeing each other and I needed some help. He wants to stay with me, but I'm afraid to let him with the trouble I'm in. He isn't safe and has nowhere to go but to Kenny O'Donnell's place. He's bored and needs a life."

"Let me see what I can come up with. You'd think Bobby would've handled this by now. Good Lord, it's been a nearly a year."

As quickly as Grandison had been captured, he'd been tossed into the dark street, wondering where he was and how he was going to get back to the morgue. Lionel wiped his mouth as he started toward the sunlit street out of the alleyway.

"My God, what the Hell was that all about?" Lionel muttered as he walked. He scratched the back of his head. He'd answered the questions he'd been asked and without comment, he had been dismissed. Just like that they had tossed him out the door and locked it. *Like I would go back in there.*

Dazed at the encounter, he continued to the sidewalk and just stood for a moment starring at the laundromat sign that would be considered part of the building he'd just been ejected from. He took out a pen and paper to jot down the name and address, thought better of it and put them back into his pocket.

I could be killed by either side now. I'd do better to keep it to myself. He thought for a moment, *No, I need to contact Kennedy and let him know. He's the one who paid for my silence; he deserves to know about this threat.* Turning in the direction of his house, Lionel Grandison had made the wise decision to go home for the day.

Chapter 5

August 12, 1964

Kenny O'Donnell sat in his office tidying up yet another stack of messy papers when the door burst open to admit a tittering Lady Bird.

"Oh, I'm so glad you're still here. I was afraid you'd left for lunch already and I really must talk to you." She fluttered into a chair in front of his desk and began removing the ever present white gloves. *A lady must always look the part,* she sighed, as she removed the enormous hat pinned to her white coiffed hair.

"Yes, ma'am." Kenny sighed and leaned toward her, "How can I help you?"

"Well it's nothing really. I just wanted your opinion on this new dress." She gestured to the frock she was wearing and waited.

"It's very becoming on you." Kenny smiled in appreciation. "Fetching."

"Do you like it, really? Lately Lyndon has been showing a decreased interest in me and I'm starting to feel neglected." Lady Bird straightened an imaginary wrinkle in her skirt.

"I'm sure he'll find you attractive, the color suits you." Kenny sighed again and leaned back in his chair. "As much as I enjoy our little chats, I really have a ton of work to do." He gestured at the pile of file folders covering his desk.

"May I have some tea?" Lady Bird asked unfazed.

"Really, Mrs. Johnson, I am swamped and must ask you to leave." Kenny stood up to help her on her way.

"Don't you want to hear about my husband's mistress?" She pouted and began putting her hat back on.

"Wait. Mistress?"

"Oh surely you know all about her, she's been with him for over twenty years now."

Christian Cafarakis finished his interview with Onassis in New York and quickly left the room. If all went well he would be the new tutor to Onassis' nearly blind son, and a mole in the household.

Hoover leaned over the desk of his Associate Director, Clyde Tolson, and tapped on the file folder on Tolson's desk, "Right here, do you see this?"

Clyde nodded and waited on Hoover to expand on the comment, "This is where it showed there was another shooter. You can barely read it but it's there. This proves that Johnson knew all along that there were two shooters. One in the book depository and one on the grassy knoll."

Hoover sat back down in the chair across from Clyde's desk. Clyde squinted to read the redacted information, which was basically a black pen marking out the passages. "So how do we prove this?"

"We'll need to talk to Warren about this report and find out what was originally in here."

"How will that help us?" Clyde leaned forward toward Hoover.

"It'll prove that Johnson at the very least knew about the scheduled assassination and at worst, was involved. After all, the route changed just prior to the actual parade. How would a shooter know where to set up if they weren't warned of the route change ahead of time?" Hoover got up. "Get Warren in here and we'll have a discussion."

Clyde nodded, "I will. I doubt he'll give anything up. He doesn't need the wrath of the President coming down on him."

Hoover smiled, "Let's at least scare him." He closed the door behind him as he left Clyde to his work.

Bill helped Norma over a fallen tree. She smiled as they released their locked hands. "I've been thinking about what you said, but I don't agree." Norma wrinkled her nose and squinted up at the sun.

"Why would you agree? You're a woman." Bill snorted.

"Smart ass. I don't agree about who was the target in this charade. It logically couldn't be me or you. Papa Doc has more to deal with right now playing detective." She stopped and leaned over to tie the cumbersome shoe string tighter around her foot. She straightened and looked up to him, "Khrushchev is worried about losing his kingdom so I don't think it was him either."

"So who are you thinking was the intended victim here, my lady?"

She grinned, "I'm working on that, but I think it might be Robert Kennedy."

Jack Lancer paced the floor at Kenny O'Donnell's house. Bobby stood in the corner nursing a high ball while Kenny was finishing a telephone conversation.

"I'm sorry, Bob. I didn't think Mary would be a problem. She's the only one I felt I could turn to."

"Now she knows you're alive and that's a huge problem." Bobby poured himself another drink.

"I don't see why." Jack pouted like a small child.

"It is only natural for you to be lost and alone. I get it, but do you not see how much danger you've put the rest of us in?" Bobby sighed and took a crumpled piece of paper from his pocket. He thrust it to Jack, who walked over to his brother and grudgingly took it.

Back off or die was printed in cut out magazine letters on a plain piece of wide ruled notebook paper.

"Cryptic," Jack handed it back to Bobby, "and sloppy."

"Yes, and to the point. It has to mean back off of Johnson and the vice presidency run or else. Johnson knows I suspect him of your death. He's avoiding me at every turn. Our best chance at catching him is to get closer to him and his cohorts."

"And now I've created another messy situation for you to deal with?" Jack hung his head.

"Exactly. Stay away from Mary Meyer."

Aristotle Onassis watched as George Joannides, CIA director in Florida over the nicknamed *Dirty Tricks* department, made his way across the pier and onto the deck of his yacht that was docked in New York.

"George, welcome to the Christina." Ari held out his hand.

"Onassis." George put his hand out and the men shook briefly. George followed him onto the deck and sat down. Ari handed him a drink, poured himself one, and sat across from him. They overlooked the water, watching as the other boats came in or sailed out.

"Have you started the rumor yet?" Onassis turned his gaze back to George.

"Of course. It was too easy to say I had heard there was a leak in the CIA office in D.C. No one likes them anyway, so my group in Florida ate it up like candy to a fat baby."

"Excellent. Now if Yuri Nosenko starts talking, we'll be safe. Damn Russian defector has lots of information that is now worth nothing." Ari gave a smug smile to George. "What about Anatoly Golitisin?"

"He'll be defecting from Russia shortly; his work with Khrushchev will be ending when the Premier is ousted. His days at the KGB are over. I've got Jim Angelton on it. He's one of our best C.I.A ops."

"So our business is concluded." Ari handed George a manila envelope filled with cash.

"As always, it is my pleasure." George placed the wad into a breast pocket as he turned and walked away.

Aristotle called out to him, "One more thing."

George turned around.

"Georgi Bolshakov needs to die."

"Defections are my field; executions are your problem." George walked off, leaving Ari staring after him in disbelief.

Johnson rolled over and tugged Madeliene Brown closer to him. He kissed her bare shoulder, an act that never had gotten old over the past two decades of their affair. She smiled and curled into him. "Lyndie," she whispered as he kissed the nape of her neck.

"Um hum?" his deep voice reverberated against her skin.

"You seem distracted. You're a little rough."

Johnson sat up and pulled the covers over them. "I'm the fucking President of the United States. That's enough to distract anyone."

"Then why did you call me to the Omni?"

"You know me all too well. I really just needed to talk and have a rough romp with my favorite gal."

"Talk first then romp." She sat up and adjusted the sheet over her as she settled back against the pillows.

"I think they're closing in. I wasn't intimidated by Onassis for a while but he knows something he can hold over me. I thought we had a deal but he's a shrewd man and will stop at nothing to get his shipping business here in the U. S." Lyndon stroked the side of her arm as he spoke.

"What are you going to do? Surely there are things you have on him. I know how ruthless you are. What about the Golden Triangle deal with the munitions? Aren't you two in business there?"

"Yes, but he wants power and he is trying to control how I make laws and what I veto to his advantage. I'm all about the money and even more about the power but I can't risk hurting America for Onassis to gain something."

"Then you must devise a way to stop him. I know you can do it, Lyndie. Have Walter help you." She stroked his hair and neck then leaned over for a long lingering kiss.

"You're right." He wrapped his arms tighter around her and pressed her into the mattress, "Now for that romp."

Castro summoned Sam Giancana with a nod. Sam walked over to the huge fireplace and looked into the cold, dead hearth.

"How are things going with our friends the Soviets?" Castro puffed on one of his cigars.

"We are on track to have him ousted by the middle of October. He won't see the New Year as the Premier." Sam lit a cigar and puffed for a moment.

"Excellent work." Castro nodded his approval, "Now, I need you to make sure Onassis is doing his part in this deal."

"I'll report back to you." Sam turned to look at Castro. "Is that all?"

"Yes. Just keep the Americans in the dark about this plot. Johnson is onboard with making sure the communists don't rule the world but he won't get what he wants. He has no idea that I would love nothing better than to control his world."

Ethel smiled as she bumped into Mary at the coffee shop.

"Oh, I'm so sorry." Ethel handed her a note as the two women feigned a casual encounter.

"I'm sorry." Mary smiled back as she tucked the note into a pocket and continued out the door.

Once in her car, Mary opened the note, *Extra security has been ordered for you. Try not to worry.* Mary crumpled the note and burned it in the car's ashtray with the built in lighter.

"I see." Barbara listened to Gregory on the opposite end of the telephone line. She puttered around the kitchen with nervous energy.

His voice filled with sympathy, "So the helicopter has been found burned. There were two bodies inside, charred beyond recognition. There's no way to tell if they were male or female. A search is underway for any survivors. I'm sorry."

"Please let me know when you find out more information. I'm just beside myself with worry." Barbara sat down on the bar stool in her kitchen when her legs suddenly refused to hold her.

"I will. Miss Hadley?"

"Yes."

"I'm sorry the news wasn't better." He sighed.

"I appreciate the update."

41

"What? Of course you're going to put me on the ticket with you!" Senator Smith yelled and then lowered her voice when her secretary poked her head around the corner into her office. She waved the annoying woman away. "I've stuck with you through all of your double dealings and supported you in this 'Vietnam' fiasco. I will most assuredly be on the ticket as your Vice President or I'll expose you."

Lyndon Johnson smiled as he played with a loose thread on his boot. He leaned back in the huge chair in the oval office and thought for a moment. "Look Margaret," he barked into the receiver, "you aren't getting a fucking choice here. You won't be on the ticket nor will you expose me. Why you may ask? Because you have too much to lose."

"With all due respect, *President Johnson,* you are the one with everything to lose. You'll be eternally sorry that you've crossed me." Senator Margaret Smith slapped the receiver down into its cradle and stormed from her office.

Chapter 6

"Holy shit this is cold water." Norma shivered in the freezing lake. Bill laughed from a discreet distance not looking. "I can do this!" She forced herself into the water.

"Why women feel the need to be clean is still a mystery to me. You look fine. We're stranded in the wilderness. Who are you trying to impress? The wildlife?" He had raised his voice a little so she could hear him.

Norma splashed icy cold water in his direction, "Nobody. I just feel gross. I don't understand why men don't care how they smell." She wrinkled her nose in disgust. *Oh what I would give for a warm bubble bath right now.*

"I have a manly, outdoorsy smell. Thank you." Bill sat on a rock, turned toward the lake, and watched her dunk her head under the water.

"Turn your back to the lake. I don't want you to watch when I get out." Norma caught him eyeing her.

As she slowly emerged from the lake he turned his back and closed his eyes. She found a grassy spot and plopped herself in the sunshine to dry. "Keep your back turned." She admonished as she made herself more comfortable.

"I will, but you sure know how to tempt a man." He grinned as he pictured the perfection of her glistening body in the sunlight. His imagination ran on until she interrupted his thoughts.

"So I was thinking...." She ignored his comment, "if the target is Bobby then it has to be one of three people; LBJ, Onassis, or Castro."

Focusing on her words, not what he thought she looked like naked, he asked, "Why just those three?"

"They make the most sense. LBJ is trying to get Bobby to back off from the vice presidency pitch, and he also hates Bobby because he knows Bobby suspects him of Jack's death. That seems like enough motive to me." Norma leaned back on her arms and starred up at the sky, "Next is Onassis. He hates Bobby because he keeps blocking his shipping business and other ventures into the U.S. He also knows Bobby despises him and wants him well away from Jackie, which is pretty strong motivation for him, as well." She reached up to fluff her hair, and turned her face up to the sun sitting quietly for a moment, gathering her thoughts.

Bill just sat there with his back turned imagining the beautiful woman behind him.

Norma broke his day dream, "Then there is Castro and the repeated attempts on his life by JFK. While Bobby has been less overt about it, he suspects that Johnson would like to see him dead. There is also the connection with Sam Giancana. Maybe he just wants information and doesn't want Bobby dead like the other two."

"I wonder sometimes who the agent is and who the civilian is." Bill smiled as he heard her struggling to get her damp body into her clothes. "Do you need some help getting dressed?"

"No thank you. I'll manage just fine alone."

"What connection does Sam Giancana possibly have with Castro?"

"Oh Bill, that is a whole different conversation."

"Tell me now."

"Giancana is a well-known mobster with ties to everyone with clout. He knows them all and he will work for anyone who will pay him well. He's a mercenary of the worst kind. One day he works for Onassis and the next he's with Castro. Sometimes he even does the same job for both men and gets paid double for it." Norma sighed as she finger-combed her hair.

"A real prince of a guy." Bill smiled as Norma approached him. "You look lovely." He leaned in to kiss her, but she moved forward.

"Let's find a good spot to camp. It'll be dark soon."

He sighed and followed her. *That woman makes me crazy!*

Anatoli Golitsin had been taken into United States custody by Jim Angelton and brought in for processing. Anatoli stood next to Jim as his paperwork went through and he was handed his papers.

"You're a free man now, Golitisin. Welcome to America."

Anatoli looked puzzled, "I'm free?"

"Yes, sir. You can thank your pal Onassis for such a smooth transition. We've got you a temporary place to stay and your money has been converted to the dollar."

Jim patted the former spy on the back and led him out of the building into the bright sunshine.

Frank waited outside the steps of the House of Representatives for Bobby to complete his meeting. He stared out over the courtyard and wished he was anywhere else at the moment.

Bobby came out with another gentleman from the House. Frank moved enough to gain Kennedy's attention. Bobby broke away from the man, lit a cigarette, and strolled toward Frank.

Frank turned and joined Bobby for a few moments.

"What are you doing here? D. C. isn't usually your style." Bobby blew out a smoke ring and stopped to let a car pass before crossing the street to the park.

Sinatra stayed with him as they entered the shaded walkway, "I've come to talk to you about the tapes. Ari wants them. He really wants them. He hit Ava Gabor hard enough to knock her off a lounger. Apparently she was told to retrieve them from you, but when that ploy failed, Onassis insisted he would get them through other means."

"You're warning me?" Bobby stopped, perplexed.

"Yes. Despite what you may think, I truly loved your brother and I have respect for the Kennedys. I thought you should watch your back." Frank slipped away before Bobby could reply.

Standing on a bridge overlooking the river, Bobby Kennedy was talking to his ally, J Edgar Hoover. "It's time to send in one of our men to get Georgi Bolshakov. The dissidents are taking over Russia and Khrushchev will be overthrown any day now."

"I could send someone." Hoover pushed his sunglasses up higher on the bridge of his nose.

"If it's all the same to you, I think I have the perfect man. He's not busy at the moment and really could use a job." Bobby smiled at the thought of Jack heading out on a simple errand and leaving his lady love to fend for herself for a few days.

"It doesn't matter to me. Just let Tolson know when it's arranged. We need to save the poor fool."

"Sam, it's time to go to Russia." Ari spoke into the crackling receiver. "Can you hear me?"

"Yes. I'll get Bolshakov and no one will ever find his body."

"Good. Let me know when you've completed the task." Ari hung up, smiling.

As Bobby opened the front door to the house, he sighed. Ethel stood there, arms crossed, toe tapping, and scowling at him with all the fury she could muster.

"Please explain to me why you've allowed me to mourn over the 'death' of your brother knowing all the while that he was safe in Switzerland." Ethel reached out and smacked him across the shoulder in rapid secession.

"Look honey…." Bobby began as he backed out of her reach. He dropped the briefcase he had been carrying and rushed at her, encircling her in strong arms effectively ceasing her ability to slap him. "I couldn't tell you or anyone. I've had to keep it a secret to protect us all. If you would have known, you would have behaved differently. I didn't want or need anyone suspecting he was alive."

"That is the lamest excuse I have ever heard!" She struggled to get out of his strong embrace. "Let me go this instant. You're not getting out of this so easily."

"You have every right to be angry but don't be mad at me. Be mad at Jack. He's the one who has caused this entire mess."

"Are you serious? 'Be mad at Jack'?" She broke free and slammed a doubled up fist into his arm with all of her might.

"Ethel, stop that right now." Bobby rubbed at his arm, "You're going to hurt yourself."

"I want to hurt *you*. Of all the low down dirty scheming you've ever done, this is the worst. I thought we were a team. I thought you trusted me." She turned and stormed off in a fury of teary anger.

Alexander and Christina Onassis sat side by side in the opulent surroundings of their home in New York City. As usual, Christina was reading to her nearly blind brother.

Christian Cafarakis entered the garden with a cart full of lemonade and cookies. "It's time for a break." He walked over to Alexander and put his hand on the boy's shoulder. Alexander stood up and allowed Christian to help him to the plush chair in the gazebo.

"What treat did you bring us today?" Alexander asked as Christina set the marker in the book and joined her brother.

"Your favorites." The teens sat down to the small treat as Christian served them.

"Where is the maid?" Christina asked sipping on her lemonade.

"She had to help with tonight's dinner party. You know your father wants everything to be perfect. I wanted a little fresh air so I offered to help out."

"I'm so glad you did!" Alexander smiled toward Christian with enthusiasm.

"Alex," Christina reprimanded, "you shouldn't show such overt affection toward our tutor."

"I'm 16 and I can choose my own friends. You need to butt out!" Alex's nostrils flared in the same way their father's did when he was angered.

"No need to get all upset about it. Just try and be more careful. You don't want anyone saying you're playing favorites, do you?"

"Really Chris, I don't care if they do. I'm so lonely here and I need a friend."

Christian had been listening to the exchange, "Of course you do. I'm glad to be your friend. You can tell me anything."

Bill jumped the ravine and held out his hand for Norma to follow, "Come on Norma. You can do it."

Exhausted, she huffed for a moment trying to catch her breath. "Give me a second. I can't make myself go any further. Besides there's something I've really got to tell you."

A sudden cracking of branches in the brush behind Bill caused them both to jump in surprise. As they watched, two Royal Canadian Mounties on horseback, appeared in the clearing.

Bill waited for a split second before crying out, "We've been rescued! Look Norma, it's the cavalry!"

Madeline lounged on the end of the bed while Lyndon buttoned up his shirt. They'd had a 'quickie' in the Omni and he was preparing to leave her.

"I hate it that you never have time for me anymore. It's been ages since we've gotten together." She pouted.

"I'm here for another moment. Do you know what it's like to run a nation? Everyone needs something from me all of the time."

"I only need something every week or so. It's been months since we had any real time together. I really liked it better when you were the Vice President."

"Look, I can only do what I can do. Can't you be happy for the few moments we get?"

"No, I don't think I can," She rolled over on the bed effectively giving him her back.

"I won't leave Mary right now. Don't you get it? They're trying to kill her." Jack blew a huge smoke ring into the air and tapped the cigarette out in the ashtray.

"You need something to get you away from here and Georgi needs to be rescued. Mary will be fine for a few days." Bobby patted Jack's shoulder. "We'll keep a close eye on her."

"Apparently I have no choice in the matter."

Bobby shook his head, "No you don't."

Jackie finished putting the last of her clothing into the suitcase. She closed the lid and snapped the latches shut. She took a look around the room making sure she hadn't left anything important.

Caroline came in, placed skinny arms around her mother's waist and sighed, "How long will you be gone?"

"Not long, darling, I'm going to go look for us a new home."

"But I like it here." Caroline moved away from her mother and plopped down on the bed.

"You'll love New York too." Jackie reached over and tussled Caroline's hair. "I'll be back before you know it."

Caroline watched her mother for another moment before asking in nearly a whisper, "Can John-John and I come too?"

"Why not? Let's go get you packed." Jackie took her daughter's hand and led her out of the room.

As Norma hobbled over toward the Mounties, a sniper shot came from the mountain, knocking him from his horse and causing the other horse to rear up on its back legs. The Mountie fell to the ground rolling into the shrubbery, holding his shoulder.

The second Mountie got his horse under control and fled in the direction of the shot. Bill thrust Norma onto the ground behind him and crouched down low while scouting the area.

A huge masked man jumped out from behind them and grabbed Norma. As she kicked and fought back, another man joined in the fight while Bill fought with three more hulking men. Bill took a hard right hook and sunk to the ground unconscious.

Two of the men flipped him over, cuffed him, and tied his legs with rope while the other men secured Norma. The wounded Mountie managed to grab one of the assailants' legs, but was roughly shaken off and kicked down the ravine.

"Help! Come back!" Norma screamed after the other Mountie, but he was heading up the mountain while the sniper fired shots at him. Suddenly the fight left her and she went limp. One of the men tossed her over his shoulder and began to hike out of the woods.

Bill moaned as two men carried him along. Norma watched for signs from Bill hoping he was biding his time before he made some brilliant move to rescue them. But he didn't stir. His head bobbed up and down as the men bounced him back and forth back up the ravine.

Chapter 7

Johnson's eyebrows rose as he listened to the man Castro had sent for a private meeting. "So you see Mr. President, I was in the book depository with your man Oswald, and I know just what transpired on that fateful day. If you wish to remain in the clear, Castro insists that you follow his plan or another American President will be dealt with accordingly."

Johnson leaned across his desk and tapped on the stack of file folders lying there. "So Brady, it comes to this? Does Castro know that you work for us too? Is he aware that you would not carry out his request because your code name 'Eugene' has been blown and the CIA knows you to be a traitor?"

Jim Brady blanched at this news, but quickly recovered, "Look, I just delivered the message. If you insist on discussing this meeting with the CIA I have my orders to kill you before I leave this office."

"As this meeting is such a secret, tell me who sent you? Castro? Giancana? That'd be my guess. He knew you could get close to me and because Castro is considered an enemy, Giancana sent you in with this reminder of my obligations. I'm well aware of them, and

I'll not be bullied by you or Castro or the CIA. You're a useless little man now. You're a traitor to your country and I could have you arrested right now for treason. OUT! Out of my office." Johnson pointed and Brady left as the President's rage grew.

Clark Clifford waltzed into the hotel bar on Madison Avenue in New York City. He glanced around for a moment and then eyed his target. As he stealthily approached, the older gentleman called for another drink.

"Onassis." Clifford muttered under his breath as fear flooded his being.

Clifford slid into the booth behind Ari and coughed lightly.

Ari raised one eyebrow and turned to see who was behind him. Clifford nodded slightly as Ari motioned for Clark to join him.

Clifford sighed and changed seats.

Ari nodded to the waitress to bring another drink and turned his attention to Clifford, "So, what's the important information you have for me?"

"It's Johnson." Clifford sat back, crossed his arms, and waited for the waitress to place the drinks in front of them. Once her swaying hips were out of sight in the darkened bar, he leaned forward, grabbed the glass, and took a swig. "He's more power mad than usual."

"He's not threatening the Golden Triangle is he?" Ari's nostrils flared.

"No, nothing like that. He wants me to eliminate Kennedy."

"Hell, I want that bastard gone too, but now is not the time. We can't afford to have anyone link the demise of Mr. Robert Kennedy to the President." Ari gulped his drink and yelled for another.

Sam arrived in Russia and headed for baggage claim. He stood waiting for his luggage as Jack Lancer left the airport with Agent Latimer and hailed a cab.

Lancer barked the address to Georgi's apartment to the cabbie. He shivered from the bone deep cold that settled over him as he lit a cigarette. Latimer watched as the cab driver slammed the trunk shut. He repeated the address and climbed in beside Jack.

"You look like you've seen a ghost." Latimer declared as Jack shook out a cigarette for him. He took it and lifted it to his lips as Lancer flipped the lighter open and flicked the flame to life.

"Maybe I did. I just have the oddest feeling that we're in for a long night."

Norma struggled against her attackers as they placed a black ski mask over her face, leaving her nose pressed tight into the fabric. Her hair stuck out of the eye sockets at the back of her head. Suddenly she was tossed onto what felt like a cot. She heard Bill moan beside her. *God, please help us get out of this mess.*

Her hands and feet were tied roughly to the cot as they began to move. *Are we in a truck?* "Where the hell are you taking us?" She screamed through the knitted ski mask.

No answer.

The vehicle bumped along an unpaved road causing the cot to move and vibrate over the floor. Norma shifted her weight back and forth trying to keep the cot upright. She heard a loud thump and metal scraping across the floor.

Apparently Bill hadn't fared as well. Suddenly, her mask was lifted enough to uncover her nose and mouth. A rough hand placed a noxious smelling cloth tightly over her nose and she was out.

Bobby looked up as Agent Stansel barged into the room breathless. "He caved." Bobby guessed.

Stansel nodded his head in the affirmative as he sat abruptly in the chair across from Bobby's desk. "Our prisoner finally caved. I guess if you starve a guy for a few days they'll do anything."

Bobby put down his pen, "Did he give you anything we can use?"

"Basically the people who hired him threatened to kill him if he spilled what he knew. He is terrified about what will happen to him and begged us to keep him in custody."

"What else?" Bobby picked up the pack, tapped out a cigarette, and lit it.

"All he knows is the targets are going to a secluded area. He thought maybe in Haiti."

"Which indicates Duvalier." Bobby frowned.

"My thoughts exactly."

Ethel picked up the mail from the side table in the hall and walked into the living room. As she leafed through the envelopes, she got a sudden chill down her spine. The envelope was addressed with letters cut out of a magazine. She dropped it and picked up the phone. Her finger trembled as she dialed.

"Bunny?" Ethel sounded hysterical, "I need Bobby to come home. Now."

Johnson sat at his desk in the Oval Office. The phone rang at his elbow. He frowned as he picked up the phone; it was a direct line that bypassed his secretary.

"Johnson." He barked into the mouthpiece of the receiver.

"What the hell do you think you're doing? How could you be so damned stupid?" Onassis snapped. Johnson leaned under the desk and turned off the tape recorder.

"What are you talking about?" Johnson sat back in his chair and gave Ari his full attention.

"The hit on Kennedy. Are you out of your mind?"

"He has to go."

"Not now you imbecile. How do you think it will look if he dies so soon after JFK?" Onassis raged at him.

"He's been getting death threats for months now. It's bound to happen sooner or later and he's not letting up on the Vice President bid. This seemed like a good solution." Johnson defended.

"I want to be rid of all of the Kennedys as much as you do but this is not the time. Do you want to jeopardize everything we've worked so hard for? The munitions going to Vietnam, the drug triangle, and the money? Back off!" Onassis slammed the phone back into the cradle for emphasis.

Jack and Agent Latimer got out of the cab in front of Georgi's apartment building. Latimer handed Jack a gun, "Don't use this unless you have to."

Latimer went first into the building, up the stairs while he glanced around at every shadow or hidden alcove. They arrived in front of the apartment and Latimer used a pick to release the lock and open the door.

Keeping close to the walls, they crept into the apartment and closed the door silently behind them. The living area and kitchen were visible from where they stood. It was empty, as was the small washroom and bedroom area.

No sign of Georgi. Latimer shrugged at Jack and motioned for him to retrace his steps.

They began to work their way out of the apartment when they heard footsteps approaching. Latimer sprinted cat-like to the eye hole in the front door and waved Jack to a window. Jack opened the glass with a mild creak and stepped onto the narrow ledge. Latimer followed and slid the window closed just as the door knob began to turn.

He side stepped out of view and held onto the bricks to keep his balance as the window curtain moved slightly. Jack was looking down at the street below. He saw a drainpipe and made his way towards it slowly with little shuffling side steps along the ledge.

Latimer heard noises inside the apartment and glimpsed a frustrated Sam in the mirror. "Go." He mouthed to Jack as he reached the drainpipe. Jack slid down as Latimer jumped for the pipe and clung to it for his life.

Sam opened the window and fired a shot at him as he managed to slide down to the ground and safety.

Norma's cot tipped over as the vehicle came to a sudden stop. She listened to the men rushing around outside and felt the rush of the cool night air as the door was thrown open. She tensed as hands grabbed her ankles and dragged her, cot and all, toward the door.

There was a scraping noise behind her and she knew that Bill was being pulled out. She heard him moan as the sound of a loud thump shook the ground. "Hey! Take it easy with him."

She received a slap across her covered face in reward for her outburst. Norma groaned and wiggled with all of her might. The grips loosened and she fell to the ground with a bruising thud.

"What the hell is wrong with you?" She screamed as she wiggled herself onto her stomach. Frantically, she pushed her face against the ground to dislodge the mask.

With a quick jerk she was pushed into a sitting position and the mask was pulled off. The sunlight nearly blinded her until the huge man blocked it out.

He leaned forward into her face, his bulbous nose pressed into hers.

"Look here, missy, you shut your mouth and follow directions before I have to hurt you."

Norma jerked her head back as his rancid breath attacked her sense of smell. She closed her eyes and simply sat with her mouth closed.

Bobby hurriedly got his things together as Bunny started to leave the office. "Did she say what was so urgent?" Bobby hollered after his secretary.

"No." Bunny tossed over her shoulder never breaking her stride. "Oh!"

Bobby watched J Edgar Hoover rush into his office brushing Bunny aside like a piece of lint.

"Kennedy, I need some answers." Hoover shut the door as he fully entered the office.

"Look Hoover, I'm in a hurry. There is an emergency at home. Ethel is frantic."

"This will only take a minute. A simple yes or no answer will get me out of here."

"Fine," Bobby sighed as he slipped on his jacket.

"Is Marilyn Monroe still alive?"

Jackie had been looking at apartments in New York City all afternoon. She was exhausted as she made her way to a small café for a cup of coffee. As she opened the door it was pulled gently from her hand. She smiled behind her to find Ari Onassis holding it open for her.

"Ari! What a pleasant surprise."

Chapter 8

August 17, 1964

Cord stood to greet Mary as she walked into the diner. "Mary, what's this all about?"

Mary slid into the booth and set her purse beside her on the bench. "Thanks for seeing me on such short notice, Cord. I'll get right to the chase. I've been followed and my house has been tossed. I need to get protection. I'm pretty sure it's the government who's after me. Can you help me?"

"What is the trouble? Why do they want you?" Cord stirred his coffee and watched her.

"I have something they want, obviously." Mary glared at him.

"Why do you think I can help you?"

"You're full of dirty little tricks, Cord, as well I know. I'm sure you could protect me if you wanted to."

"Why should I?"

"Because I have information in my diary about you as well. If they get it, you'll be exposed, too. Blackmail isn't beyond me right now. I'm desperate."

Bobby rushed into the house to find Ethel in the den staring at an unopened envelope with magazine letters pasted to form the name and address. It was sitting on the sofa beside her. He put his things down on the recliner and walked over to the sofa. He gently sat beside her as he moved the letter out of her sight.

"Bobby? What is it?"

"You know what it is, honey." Bobby took her into his arms as he stroked her hair softly.

"Will they get to you? Will they succeed?" Ethel raised her worried face and met his eyes.

"No, honey. They won't get to me or to us."

"How can you be so certain?"

"Look, whoever did this is a crack pot. They couldn't even spell 'Kennedy' with two n's. Don't you worry about this letter. I'll give it to the secret service and have them check it out. We're not even going to open it."

"But I'm so afraid. You know how I love you."

"I know, honey." He kissed the top of her forehead, "I promise it'll be all right."

Lancer and Agent Latimer rushed around a corner and into a cab. They sped off as Sam reached the end of the street, gun shining in the moonlight.

"We don't have much time. We have to find Georgi before that goon does. We want him alive but I'm not so sure about Sam." Lancer leaned back, took the pack of cigarettes out of his pocket, and shook out one.

"I think he may be hiding in a dacha, a little house outside of town. It's common for privileged Russians to keep a dacha in the country for summer. Do you know if he had one?" Agent Latimer held out his hand as Jack shook a cigarette into it.

"No, but I think it's likely that Khrushchev has one, and he would have access too. He could have secreted

Georgi away for safety. Let's go see Khrushchev." Lancer put the cigarette to his lips and lit it.

Latimer gave the address to the cabbie.

Clark Gifford sauntered into the Oval Office and sat across from the President. It took Johnson a minute to look up.

"What the hell do you want?"

"As you know, we've been watching Mary Meyer for some time now. It has come to our attention that the diary she keeps contains information that you don't want known to the public."

"What kind of information?" Johnson leaned over his desk.

"She apparently knows what happened to JFK and has some interesting theories on who was behind it. She even mentions your code name, Volunteer, along with several drawings of what probably happened. She's too damn close to the truth to let it be." Gifford smiled as he awaited the answer he knew would come.

"Kill her."

Jackie and Ari followed the waitress to a little window table and ordered coffee. Jackie removed her light jacket and placed her purse primly on top of it. "What brings you to New York?"

"Darling, you know I spend a good deal of time in the city. I'm here on business. I've brought the children with me this time. They're wanting to go to some Broadway Show and of course Christina wants to go shopping. I detest that sort of thing." Ari leaned back in his chair. "You look better."

Jackie crinkled her brows together, "Is that a compliment?"

Ari laughed, took her small hand in his, lifted it to his lips and kissed it. "Of course darling, you know how I hate a woman who looks like a circus elephant."

"That's not flattering." Jackie pulled her hand away with a slow deliberateness.

"You know I think you're gorgeous. I'm glad I ran into you today. I'm having a huge party on Friday night and would love to have someone of your caliber in the mix. Can you make it?"

"It's short notice but I think I can manage an appearance."

"Do you think you could get some of your famous friends to attend? I want to improve my standing here in the city and some local royalty would certainly be a boost."

"Now Ari, why should I help you?" Jackie smiled flirtatiously.

"Because, darling girl, I've given you thousands of dollars in gifts as well as cash. Do I need to explain further?"

Jackie's smile faded, "No. I'll see who I can persuade to attend."

"That's my girl." Ari stood up, tossed a fiver on the table, kissed the top of her head and walked away.

Mary Meyer strolled into the department store with her purse tucked under her arm. Cord snuck up behind her and grabbed her around the waist.

"Help!" Mary shrieked as Cord laughed, twirled her around, and laughed at her reaction. "You're way too skittish. Why someone would think you were afraid of your own shadow."

Mary slapped him hard across the face. "How dare you mock me? You know damn well that I'm being stalked."

"Oh come on, Mary. Is the boogie man going to jump out and eat you?" Cord laughed. "Or maybe the agency?"

"I know that you work for Aristotle as well as the CIA and that makes you terrifying."

Cord lowered his head as he pulled her up close to him. "Watch out Mary, I've found out what's really going on. You *should* be afraid. I'll do what I can to protect you, but this is serious."

"I doubt that. I wouldn't trust you not to put a bullet in my head if it would earn you enough money."

"No. I do still love you. Anyone else and you'd be right. But not you, never you." Cord released her and left her standing there, confused.

Jose Fuegos paced the office of Fidel Castro terrified. Castro stood behind his desk, hands firmly planted on the wood and breathed in a deep breath.

Jose stopped and turned around to face Castro.

"She's out of reach? How can you fucking tell me Marita, the one who so evilly betrayed me, is out of reach?" The dictator came out from behind his desk and stood in front of the now shaking Jose.

"It's not my fault. The U.S government has her in hiding. I can't find her and even if I did they'd never let me close enough to kill her."

"Perhaps." Castro agreed, "But someone must pay for this outrage. If it isn't Marita perhaps it should be you?"

Norma watched as they sat Bill up and jerked off the ski mask. He groaned and blinked against the sun. He slowly looked around and saw her. He winked and gave her a weak grin. Bill was jerked to his feet about the same time Norma was. The ropes were cut from their ankles and they were pushed down a steep, snowy slope toward a small abandoned shack made of tin roofing and clapboard walls.

Opening the wooden door, the men shoved them inside. They were unceremoniously stuffed roughly into chairs where they had their feet tied to each chair leg and their hands tied awkwardly to the back rest of the chair. Norma squirmed to get more comfortable as the men left, closing the heavy wooden door behind them.

The room was dark now that the door was closed, except where the sun filtered through tiny holes in the clapboard walls. Norma fidgeted and began to get cold.

"Be still. You'll only tire yourself out."

Norma wiggled, struggling against the ropes and finding a little warmth in the movement. "Are you okay Bill?"

"I'll be fine." She could hear his smile.

"Where do you think we are?"

"Still in Canada. I'm guessing but I wouldn't swear to it. What little terrain we saw suggests we're in the Rockies. It certainly explains the snow."

"What are we going to do?" Norma sounded panicked.

"We're going to play nice and wait for dark."

"Then what?"

"Then we can try and work our way out of the ropes. For now, try to rest. I've got one hell of a headache."

"Bill?"

"Yes?"

"There's something I have to talk to you about."

Christian Cafarakis let the phone ring three times then hung up. He immediately dialed again. The receiver on the other end was picked up immediately.

"What's up?"

"Onassis is having a huge party in New York this Friday and he's invited Jackie."

"I'm on it." Kenny O'Donnell hung up the phone and leaned back in his chair as he swung his feet onto the desk. "I'll get you my pretty and your little dog too!" he laughed as he lit a cigarette, twirled the roll-a-dex, then picked up the secure phone and dialed.

Barbara Hadley sat nervously at the diner waiting on Gregory Morris to meet her. She shredded a few paper napkins and was sweeping away the mess when he sat down across from her.

"Oh!" Barbara turned scarlet as she moved the pile out of the way. "I was just . . . ."

Gregory laughed at her, "I do the same with a cigarette. That makes a much bigger mess."

Barbara relaxed a little, "How are you?"

"I'm doing fine. I'm thinking about retiring soon." Gregory signaled the waitress and ordered a cup of coffee.

"What will you do if you retire?" Barbara stirred her own coffee and added an unneeded sugar packet.

"Perhaps find a beach and fish all day. But you wanted information on your friend. I can't tell you much. They've been spotted alive in the Canadian mountains where the Royal Mounties tried unsuccessfully to pick them up. One of the Mounties was shot and the other was chasing the sniper who fired at them. Apparently they've been taken by several masked assailants, but we've no more information at the moment." Gregory accepted the coffee from the waitress and waved her away.

Barbara sat forward so abruptly that she spilled her coffee. "Holy Mother! Who do you think took her?"

"The better question is, who do *you* think took her?" He stirred sugar into his coffee.

"I think it had to do with either Onassis or Duvalier. Both have reasons to want her. I don't know that Onassis is the problem so much though. He may just a have a small interest." Barbara smiled, "I'm rattling on, aren't I?"

"It's fine. It's called processing. We take into account different reasons why someone would want to do this and then rule them out."

"Then I would look to Papa Doc if I were investigating."

Chapter 9

August 19, 1964

Bill struggled to push his chair back against Norma's. After several minutes of pushing and hopping in little spurts, he managed to get close enough to her to bruise her knuckles with a chair rung. Norma grunted but said nothing as they managed to grasp hands.

Papa Doc hurried through the door and into the cold room. He closed the door behind him and turned his full attention to the two people tied to chairs ten paces away from him.

He flipped on the light and smiled as they both blinked at the sudden brightness disorienting them.

"Well, well, well!" Papa Doc approached Norma. "At last I've got you!" He reached down and lifted her chin so that he could see her face fully. "You lying bitch. You've been nothing but trouble to me since I found out who you were."

Norma sat quietly as her entire body began to shake.

"What do you want with us?" Bill demanded.

Papa Doc laughed, then turned to Bill with a hiss, "Stay out of this if you want to live." He kicked Bill's chair over on its side for emphasis.

He turned his full attention to Norma, "I know you are Marilyn Monroe, I've watched you and I KNOW." He raised his hand high and prepared to hit her, "Do you deny it?"

Norma sat still and whispered, "No." He slapped her hard enough to make her fall backwards. The chair leaned at a crazy tilt against the flimsy wall. He pulled her back upright with a crazed light gleaming in his eye. He smacked her across the face once more. She spit blood out of her mouth onto his shirt. He stomach-punched her and yelled. "Say it again, bitch. Tell me your name."

"Marilyn Monroe." She held her head up defiantly.

"I KNEW it!" Papa Doc danced wildly around the room. "I've got you. I've finally got you. Now Onassis will know that I'm not crazy."

"What are you going to do with us?" Bill demanded.

Papa Doc stopped dancing and turned to Walton, "I haven't decided, but one thing is clear, I don't have any use for you at all. So shut your mouth."

"What about John Kennedy? Is he dead?"

Norma kept her mouth closed, her head down, and her eyes shut. The invariable hit knocked her chair to the ground. She struggled to bring the chair upright, but it was no use with the ropes keeping her securely in place.

Papa Doc stormed out of the room, slammed the door closed, and hollered for the guard, "Stand here and don't move! I need to think about this."

Georgi Bolshakov sat in the garden listening to the farmers bringing in the harvest. He leaned forward and took his cup from the table and sipped a weak tea.

A strange noise had him twist around just in time to see Agent Latimer jump from behind a scrawny tree, gun pointed right at Georgi, as Jack moved out from behind a small building.

"Jack!" Georgi rushed to greet Lancer with a bear hug. "I thought you were dead."

Jack smiled and returned the embrace. "I am, my friend, and you will be too if we don't get out of here."

Latimer holstered the gun and led them back to the waiting car.

"Hoover here." J. Edgar leaned back in his leather chair and tapped a pencil on his notepad while he held the receiver with the other hand.

"Mr. Hoover, I'm with the RCM and wanted to let you know that I have found your missing agent."

"And you are?" Hoover leaned forward and pressed both hands on the phone's receiver.

"Pardon my manners. I'm Constable Kevin Parsons. I was able to track them from the helicopter crash site. Two of my men were in the process of rescuing them when they were shot at by at least one sniper. We lost them, temporarily, as one of the Mounties was shot off his horse."

Hoover snapped, "Details man! Time is of the essence."

"He'll recover, thank you for asking," Constable Parsons continued, "They were taken to a small abandoned farm house up near Barrier Lake."

"Is that where they are now? Why didn't you idiots rescue them?" Hoover stood up, knocking his chair backward into the credenza behind him. He paced a few short steps around his desk.

"Mr. Hoover, we've overheard that they are being transported to a party that apparently. . . ." Constable Parsons paused to double check his notes, "Mr. Onassis is having in New York this Friday evening."

Hoover slammed the phone down without thanking the good constable for the valuable intel he had just shared.

Ari sneered as Johnson came toward him, looking nervous and glancing about like a guilty child stealing money from his mother's purse. Johnson reached the park bench Ari was sitting on. He paced in front of Onassis.

"How dare you call me to meet you here? I'm calling the shots now." The President composed himself and sat beside Onassis.

"Oh really? Do you forget that we're partners in this scheme? How dare you order Kennedy removed? Did you not barely escape the public's noose during the last death of a Kennedy?" Onassis glared at him. "Let me make something extremely clear to you. I, and I alone am in charge here. You are but a pathetic pawn in my game. If *you* don't want everyone in America to know that you placed the man on the grassy knoll, then you will not pursue the elimination of another Kennedy until I say it is time."

Johnson, President of the United States through default, blanched as Onassis' words left him terrified and unable to defend himself.

Onassis let his words sink in for a moment, noticed the silence of his bench mate, and continued, slowly, clearly and with deadly calm, "The party is set for Friday night. You will have all of the potential backers at that party or else I will expose you for the arrogant asshole you are."

Kenny picked up the ringing phone and pressed "1" for the line. "O'Donnell here."

"Kenny, it's Christian. I have that guest list you asked for. Also Onassis has rented a mansion in the Hamptons for the event."

O'Donnell began jotting down names as Christian spouted them off.

"Thanks!" Kenny rang off.

Gregory slipped his arms around Barbara's waist. He nuzzled her lips with his until they naturally melded into a deep, passionate kiss. He pulled his lips away from hers with a sigh, "It's nice to see you too!"

Barbara laughed and placed her head against his shoulder, wrapping her arms tighter around his still somewhat slim waist. "Did you miss me, then?"

"Sassy, aren't you?" Gregory pushed back from her in order to see into her laughing eyes. "Maybe I won't tell you the news I've brought you then."

Barbara pulled out of his arms and took a step back, "Is it Norma? She's dead isn't she? I just knew it." She began wringing her hands and fell into a heap in the high backed chair behind her.

Gregory knelt beside her, "No, she's not dead. She's alive and on her way back to New York."

Barbara began to cry in earnest. She pulled him close to her, "Oh thank you, God! That poor woman has been through so much."

"Wait until I tell you what's going on." Gregory handed her a handkerchief and waited until she blew her nose.

Marita and Clint Hill heard the front door crash open as men in masks began pouring into the house. "Run! Go to the safety zone. I'll have someone there to meet you at nine tonight."

Clint shoved her out of the nearest window. He watched her take off and then jumped out the same window, hunched under it, and waited for the unlucky soul who tried to look out of it.

"You're mad, aren't you?" Norma watched Bill. The guard had come in and righted her chair. Papa Doc had been cruel, accusing, and worst of all, revealing.

"Yes." Bill stared at her, really seeing her, looking her over in an effort to see her for the first time.

"In all fairness, I've been trying to tell you for ages." Norma sighed, "It's such a crazy story and I never dreamed I'd fall in love with anyone. It does seem a bit ludicrous once one is deceased."

Bill snorted in laughter despite his anger.

"That's better." Norma smiled at him with her dazzling, 'I'm a star' smile.

"I can't believe I never put it together." Bill shook his head. "Some sleuth I am."

"Well, how could you? I do resemble the star I once was, but I have worked on finding me. There's little of the woman I once thought was so important left in me anymore. Please forgive me, Bill."

"You love me?" Bill sputtered.

"Yes."

"Of course I forgive you!"

They smiled at one another aching to embrace, but still tied up. Bill sighed in frustration, "Okay, now I teach you how to get out of tied ropes as if by magic."

"What? How?"

"The CIA has a book, a secret book, The Official CIA Manual of Trickery and Deception. It was written, in part by Mullholland, the famous magician. He taught us how to use the sleight of hand tricks on a grander scale. Now listen closely."

"Just one question," Norma stopped trying to learn the trick for a moment, "If we're being taken to New York, why are we escaping now?"

"We're not. We are just getting ready for our escape in New York. A good agent plots and plans until the time is right to pounce."

"We have to attend." Bobby looked sternly at the distraught Ethel.

"I hate that Greek idiot. He's been trying to win over Jackie since before Jack died, I mean, left." Ethel threw up her hands, "I don't know what I mean anymore."

"While our sentiments toward Onassis are the same, we are still going. Jackie invited us and I need to be there to make sure Marilyn is rescued. I've got Latimer and Stansel working the logistics. We've only got a small window to get them back before Duvalier reveals that she's alive and demands to know where Jack is. I'm sure she hasn't given up his whereabouts or she'd be dead by now."

"I'll do it for Norma. You owe me a nice trinket for this favor." Ethel smiled, knowing she would get an expensive trinket in exchange for her cooperation.

"I'm glad your affection for Marilyn is motivation enough because you certainly don't seem too concerned about doing it for me." Bobby patted her rump as he made his way out of their bedroom.

Hoover stood admiring himself in the mirror. It wasn't often he allowed himself to get all dressed up, but tonight he was celebrating. He turned and looked more closely at his left side and then the right. *"Yes, I think this will do nicely."* He smiled at his reflection, added a touch more lipstick, and straightened the skirt on his party dress. *I hope Clyde likes it.* He stooped over, picked up his purse, turned off the light, and closed the door with a smile. *It should be a lovely evening at the Omni.*

Marita hunkered under the football stands in the quiet stadium of a High School in Palo Alto, CA. She listened for the bird-call that would save her from spending the rest of her life in hiding. Castro had been getting too close in finding her lately.

She heard the call and made a soft mewing noise in response. As promised the call came again, and the agent stepped out of the shadows into a slim sliver of light from the moon. Marita stepped out from under the bleachers just as the shots rang out. Mortified, she hurried back to her shelter as she watched the unarmed agent fall.

The private jet landed in Manassas, Virginia and taxied up the runway. Jack starred out the window for a moment before he turned to Georgi. "Welcome back."

"Some thrill. At least I'm not dead." Georgi sighed, placing his forehead against the cool glass window.

"I know it's not the luxurious lifestyle that you are accustomed to, but I've heard Alvictus, the safe house, is nice. Alice, the landlady, is wonderful. You'll love her." Latimer chimed in as the plane rolled to a stop at the gate. A sleek black limo awaited the trio as they cleared the steps of the plane.

"I may be joining you. Bobby hasn't said it yet, but I know somewhere like this is where I'm going to end up."

"We could have lots of good times then, right Jack?" Georgi tried for a smile. "I hate water. Did I ever tell you that? Now I'm living by a lake in a country that hates me."

"I tell you what. I'll convince Mary to give up her job and we can come live at Lake Jackson with you. We can talk over the good ole days when we were both loved and needed." Jack patted his friend on the back and then watched him get into the limo. The driver stood back from the open door so Jack could lean in for a final goodbye. "I'm sure she'd feel much safer here than in D.C."

Chapter 10

August 22, 1964

"Stansel, where are we on those tapes?" Bobby tapped his long finger against the side of his cheek as he waited on the reply.

"I've got two more to finish. Right now it's all about getting fired from *Something's Gotta Give*, her new house, ordering lawn chairs from Mexico, and her stupid girl crisis'. There's not enough information on there to discern when her next hair appointment is let alone the secrets Onassis is hoping to discover."

Bobby leaned back in his chair and steepled his fingers. "Thank you for coming in and giving me this update."

"I'll have the others finished by the end of the month. There were several conversations between her and John F Kennedy. What surprised me is the ruthless way he dumped her. Why did you do his dirty work?"

"Look, Stansel, we're a close family and we cover for each other. Just remember that whatever else you hear on those tapes is strictly confidential, and must remain that way." Bobby stood up suddenly and Stansel nearly jumped, but he composed himself and kept his gaze locked on Kennedy's.

"Of course." Stansel stood, shook Kennedy's hand, and left the room.

"Marilyn, I need you to watch this." Bill was standing in the middle of the shack while Norma watched out for the guards marching the premises.

She turned to him, startled to hear her name. "It's been a long time since I've been called that."

Bill grinned, "Don't you like it?"

"I've gotten pretty used to being Norma Baker. I think I'll keep it."

"Okay, Norma, I need you to watch this. I'm going to teach you some moves to get away from an attacker. I'm also going to show you exactly where to put the palm of your hand on a person's nose to shove it up into his brain."

Norma winced as she watched him explain his movements. Then she got up and he demonstrated them on her. They were in the middle of one maneuver when they heard the guards talking outside.

"I'll check them this time." The guard opened the door just as they got their hands back into the loosened knots on the ropes. From all appearances they were still tied up.

The guard looked at Norma, "Do you need to relieve yourself for the night?"

She shook her head no. She looked down at her lap and not at the guard.

"It seems like you never have to pee. Are you part camel?" He turned to Bill who also shook his head.

The guard closed the door without another word. They sighed with relief. "That was close. I'll need to be more careful." Bill stood up and gestured for Norma to follow. They continued where they'd left off. "You're a natural at this."

Norma smiled, "It's all about acting and mimicking. I can do that."

Jose Fuegos sat nervously watching as Castro fiddled with his loaded pistol. "I asked you to do one thing. You have failed." Castro glared at Fuegos.

"It's true that my men have been unable to locate her, but it is not a lost cause. We shot an agent, but didn't apprehend her in California. I'm sure my men will succeed." Fuegos shifted in his seat as Castro continued to glare at him.

"It is no longer a matter of your concern." Castro lifted the pistol with practiced ease and shot Fuegos cleanly through the left eye socket.

Aristotle opened the closet doors as Jackie stood watching. She'd sent the children off with the nanny for some ice cream. He sighed and shook his head, "None of these gowns are right for the party." He slammed the doors closed and moved to the living area of the suite. He poured himself a drink and sat down on the love seat.

"Ari, we need to talk about something serious." Jackie moved next to him onto the love seat and crossed her ankles primly.

"Don't worry darling, just charge the dress to me. In fact, I'll call Jean Desses. All of my mistresses love her clothes. She'll know exactly what I want." Ari waved with a dismissive gesture.

"It's not that. I need to talk to you about Jack." She shifted uncomfortably on the loveseat.

"What more do you possibly need to say on this subject?" Ari stood up and refilled his drink. He lit a cigarette with impatience, sucked up a lung full, and blew it out with savage intensity.

"I know we've agreed it's a taboo subject, but that's the problem. John is still alive."

"Jackie, you were there pulling his brains off of the trunk of the limo when he was shot. I still think you escaped public scrutiny on that ridiculous move. I mean most people would have dove for safety, but not you! You climb OUT of the car onto the back to retrieve brain matter." Ari blew another smoke ring.

"I knew better than anyone that I wasn't the target and the shooting was over. I had no reason to fear because I know that you and Johnson were behind it. Perhaps it was rather stupid, but I really didn't think about it. I just kept thinking he needed the rest of his skull."

"Sometimes you baffle me," he struck her across the face. "I believe you are an intelligent woman and then you do something like that. You verbalize what we've agreed must never be said. But," he stroked her face and kissed her cheek where he'd struck her, "the world must think you're a truly devoted wife, hey lover?"

"I was as devoted as he was." Jackie stood, clearly miffed. "I'm trying to tell you that what you think of my behavior doesn't matter because the man in the limo was NOT JACK."

Hoover sat at his desk, tapping a pencil against the file for Marilyn Monroe. His conversation with Bobby still rattled him.

"Is Marilyn Monroe still alive?" Hoover asked.

Kennedy had stared at him for a brief moment before his hurried reply, "Yes and John is too."

Bobby had rushed out of the office to go home to his apparently hysterical wife.

He rubbed his nose with an index finger and his thumb. "If it's true that John Kennedy is alive he's still the President. Why didn't he say anything to anyone? Who was in that car?"

He pressed a button on his telephone panel, "Tolson, get in here."

Jack sat in Kenny O'Donnell's house watching his brother pace the room. After a few moments, Bobby stopped in front of him. "I know you want to be with Mary, but that's not a good idea. She's being watched. Having it discovered that you are alive is not on the agenda."

"Mary understands me. You don't. I need someone to love me. Jackie won't even let me see the children from a distance."

"Do you fucking hear yourself? You've lost your mind. Of course you can't see the children or Jackie or anyone! No, you're going with Latimer to find Marita before Castro kills her."

Lady Bird flittered around her house wondering if she'd done the right thing. All she ever wanted was to have a good relationship with her husband, but Madeleine Brown had been a usurper for 20 years or more. *That nice Mr. O'Donnell has been so understanding and helpful. He's always so nice.*

She went into the bedroom she shared with Lyndon and opened her closet. She looked at the prim, matronly clothing suitable for the wife of the president and sighed. *Jacquelyn is always stylish and elegant while I look like I'm one hundred years old. No wonder Lyndon finds me boring. Just for one day I would love to be free and wild.* She sighed, grabbed a fashion magazine from the end table, and headed out the door.

Sam Giancana had arrived in New York City with trepidation. Onassis was meeting him at a coffee shop.

As the taxi pulled up in front of the café, Giancana felt dread rise up in his throat.

He entered the shop and ordered a coffee from the waitress as he waited for Onassis. It had been a long journey and exhaustion began to make his shoulders sag.

Onassis strode in and plopped down in the booth sitting across the table from Sam.

"Georgi got away. I saw him getting in a car with the feds. I was just moments behind, but I was too late." Giancana blurted as soon as Ari was settled.

"It's okay. Our mole will take care of anything he might say. I have much bigger worries right now." Onassis waved away the waitress and stood up to leave.

"Can I do anything to help you?" Giancana stared up at him.

"Not now. I'll call you." Ari left as quickly as he'd come.

Lyndon Johnson stormed out of the Oval Office, screaming for his secretary. "Where the hell are you?"

The harried lady came running with an armful of files, pen tucked in her bun and a coffee mug in the other hand. "Yes, Mr. President?"

"I need you to get me Jenkins right now! Can't you do anything?"

She rushed to the phone and called Jenkins. He was only next door. "He'll be right here, Mr. President."

Walter rounded the corner a few seconds later.

"Jenkins, thank God you're here. My world is crumbling and only you can fix it." LBJ ushered him into his office and slammed the door closed.

"Don't you think it's odd that we haven't seen Duvalier since the initial interrogation?" Norma asked early Friday morning.

"It does seem off. I heard the guards say we were being moved today. New York I believe."

Norma glanced over at Bill. He was staring out of the crack in the clapboard. "New York?"

Bill nodded and placed a finger to his lips. They quickly resumed the *position* as two guards came into the room.

Cord stood next to the tall window overlooking Central Park as he waited on Onassis to finish his phone conversation. Ari hung up the receiver, "Come on over here and have a seat."

Cord did as he was instructed and sat in a chair across the massive desk that Onassis had brought with him from Greece. "Mary is a smart woman. I think she has either discovered, or she's really close to finding out, that I work for you and I'm trying to get the diary from her."

"You must find that diary. There is too much at stake here to wonder about what that diary says. I need you to get it no matter how you achieve it."

"Senator Smith, I tried to stop him." The young aide was beet red and struggling to hold a determined Clark Clifford at bay.

Margaret nodded for him to come in and the aide backed away, straightened her skirt, and shut the door behind her.

"To what do I owe this unannounced pleasure?" Senator Smith closed an open manila file folder on her desk and placed it in the out-box.

"I've come on behalf of President Johnson." Clifford continued to stand as he leaned over the desk mere inches from her face. "He would like me to impart to you the importance of rescinding your kind offer to be his vice presidential running mate. While the offer is somewhat unrealistic, it has emphatically been denied. Any further conversation on this matter will be dealt with in a swift and rather final manner." Clifford stood up straight as he watched her face. "I see that I've made myself clear."

He turned on his heel and left her sitting there speechless, closing the door silently as he exited.

Lady Bird stood in the dressing room starring at her reflection in the mirror. The boutique owner had cautioned her against this particular dress. "Are you sure madam? This is usually a gown worn to a high school prom."

Chapter 11

Mary continued to run through the heavily treed park towards home. She could hear the tree branches swishing and the ground cracking as she ran for safety. The men came crashing through a bush and the pop! pop! pop! of gunfire whizzed past her. She turned and ran in short zig zags as Cord had taught her. *I hope that he's right and they won't hit me this way.*

She continued on until she reached a big open garage door. Mary slid inside and listened to the men storm past her hiding place. She slipped to the floor, breathing hard, nearly crying in relief.

<u>August 23, 1964</u>

Bobby entered his office and noticed the sealed envelope on his desk. He opened the envelope, spilling the sheet of paper onto the blotter. It was from O'Donnell.

Party goers
LBJ

Lee Radziwill
New Hampshire Senator McIntyre
Ted Kennedy
Maria Callas
Prince Rainier
King of Saudi Arabia
George Papadopoulos
Cary Grant
Adam Clayton Powell
Ralph Yarborough
Patrick McNamera
Location: a leased mansion in the Hamptons

He smiled and slid the list back into the envelope. Sitting at his desk, he prepared to deal with the day ahead.

Jack Lancer and Agent Latimer leaned against the car eating hot dogs they'd purchased from a cart on Venice Beach, California. They watched the people walk along the beach or frolic in the water. Both men were dressed in board shorts, t-shirts, and running shoes. Latimer's shirt was baggier than he needed and the wind showed the outline of the gun tucked in the back of his shorts.

Jack leaned back further on the car and crossed his feet in an attempt to be casual, "You know Wes, we've been working together a lot lately. Do you really think that Marita will show up at a busy beach from a crazy advertisement in the paper?"

Latimer straightened up, and pulled down his government issued sunglasses. "Yes I do. Otherwise, I wouldn't be standing here eating this disgusting hot dog and dealing with a man who, for all intents and purposes, is dead."

Jack laughed, a hardy, deep belly laugh that surprised Wes. "I'm actually serious. I didn't realize I had signed up for baby-sitting duty when I joined the agency."

"Are you married?" Jack finished off his hot dog and sipped at his can of soda.

"No."

"Ever had a family?"

"Look Lancer, it's not your business. . ." Latimer began and stopped short, "It's her."

He nodded his head toward the beach where a young woman was strolling along the surf. She was wearing a giant straw hat with a large purple flower tucked behind her left ear, the signal. "Let's go get our girl."

Latimer pushed away from the car, tossed the remains of his hot dog in a nearby trash container as they casually headed toward the water and then veered to the left to avoid the tide.

J. Edgar Hoover and Clyde Tolson sat in the conference room at the Federal Bureau waiting for Earl Warren to answer. He had been sitting with his hands folded in his lap staring at the wall for a good five minutes.

Hoover had enough of his silence, "Warren! I need you to answer the question. Let me repeat it for you. How many bullets were in John F. Kennedy?"

Warren continued to stare at the wall. Hoover got up and walked around to where Earl was sitting. "I can have you arrested. Now please answer the question."

Warren looked up into the angry face of Hoover, "One."

"Bullshit! The Zapruder film shows that he is forced backward as something strikes him in the neck, and then he is jerked forward as the shot from Oswald enters the back of his head. How then, can there have only been one bullet?"

Warren starred back at the wall. "I'm not at liberty to answer your questions. If you'd like more information you can read the report. I believe you have the full copy."

"The full fucking copy is so redacted you can't read anything of importance, except for one thing. At one point it clearly says there were two bullets that struck the President. How do you explain your answer of just one bullet?" Hoover took a deep breath and sat down in the seat next to him, leaving Clyde at the head of the table alone.

Warren sighed, "Look, if you want those questions answered, it's above my pay grade. I couldn't tell you even if you did put me in prison, starve me, or torture me. I have orders."

Clyde had been silent during the interview. He got up and brought Warren a fresh cup of coffee. He set the cup down in front of Earl and handed him the sugar bowl and creamer. "Look, Earl, we've known each other for quite some time. We're just trying to get a few things straight. This interview is strictly confidential. It stays between the three of us."

"True." Hoover agreed.

Warren thought this over as he sipped the hot coffee. "I still don't know if I should talk to you or not. This is a directive from the President himself."

"Johnson?" Hoover glanced toward Clyde. "Why would he give you an order? Wasn't your commission set up to find out the truth about the assassination?"

Johnson plopped into his chair as Jenkins took a seat across from him. "What is the issue here?"

"Everything is imploding at once. Robert Kennedy won't get off this idea that he is going to be my running mate. Onassis is whining about the Golden Triangle. No one likes me and all of the voters think it's a bad idea to escalate this conflict."

"First of all, you have the power to choose your own running mate. Who do you want it to be?"

"Hubert Humphrey."

"Then announce that sitting Cabinet members won't be considered. You can move him to the very end of the convention and name Humphrey early on so you're done with it. It's not rocket science. Once you have named your guy all Kennedy can do is smile graciously and congratulate him."

"Walter! You're brilliant." Johnson leaned forward and slapped his knee. "That's a load off. Onassis told me I can't do away with Kennedy so soon after we got rid of his brother."

"He has a valid point. Now, what's the matter with the triangle?"

"We have to make sure that all of the drugs are run to Cambodia, Laos, and Vietnam as well as the munitions or we will lose everything."

"I'll work on that. You stop worrying so much. That is why I'm here." Walter stood up. "Is there anything else, Mr. President?"

"Not at the moment. Thank you, Jenkins. I'd fall apart if it weren't for you."

Mary knocked frantically on Ethel Kennedy's door. She was dusty and tired after her night in that empty garage, and she desperately needed help. A maid answered and led her through the house to the backyard where Ethel was dealing with children running through a water sprinkler attached to the hose.

Ethel saw Mary and waved her over. "You'd think with that huge in ground pool that we'd be playing there, but these goofy children saw this on Television and now the pool is boring to them."

Mary laughed nervously and cleared her throat. "I'm so sorry to come here, but I don't know where else to go. I was nearly killed last night and I've been hiding out all morning in someone's garage."

"It isn't good for you to be here. If anyone knows you've come, we'll all be dead." Ethel frowned at Mary, then grinned. "I would have done the same thing." She patted Mary's hand.

"I'm sorry. I don't want to put you or your family in more danger. I just need a direction. Where can I hide?"

Ethel wrinkled her forehead. "Didn't you tell Cord you needed protection? I've informed O'Donnell and he assured me someone would be assigned to you."

"Let's go with no one so far." Mary leaned back into the lawn chair. "Cord is less than useless. He's playing both sides and I can't trust him."

"Are you hungry?" Ethel watched Mary nod in the affirmative. "Let's feed you, then we'll figure out where you can hide until dark. I've got room in this hulking old place. If no one saw you come here, we should be safe and if they did, we will know soon enough."

"Thank you." Mary sighed her relief and closed her eyes while Ethel ordered some sandwiches to be brought out to them.

"Why hasn't someone been attached to me?"

Ethel shook her head, "I couldn't really say. I've been assured that you'd have protection. They were supposed to be assigned to you before the weekend."

"We've got a mole in the works and I know it's not Cord despite his double dealings." Mary sighed and closed her eyes.

Ethel didn't respond. She was silent for a moment before asking, "Did you see any secret service men when you came up?"

"Yes, I had to show my identification before they'd let me in."

"What? Why didn't you tell me when you first got here?" Ethel leaned toward Mary. "They all know you're here. It's not safe. I'll have the car pulled around and we'll sneak you out of here in the trunk. Just eat quickly while I inform the driver of our plan. Don't worry, he adores me and will keep his mouth closed." Ethel stood up to leave her as the sandwiches were placed on the table at her elbow. "Wrap some of those up and cram them in your purse. You have to go. NOW."

Jim Angelton stood near Cord Meyer at the usual meeting place. They were looking out at the river and smoking. "I lost her." Jim blew a smoke ring into the warm air.

"What?" Cord turned to him.

"I lost her in the suburbs. She was there, running down the alley one minute and the next, she was just gone. Vanished." Angelton blew another smoke ring and frowned down into the river.

"Damn it! That's a trick I taught her. Maybe you and I should discuss some of her maneuvers so she'll be an easier target next time."

"We tossed her house again. No sign of the diary. Where do you think it might be?" Angelton kept staring down at the water.

"Maybe at her office. I'm sure she knows we're not going to give up on her house. She won't say or do anything there that will give us a single clue. She's good. She should have joined the force." Cord threw his cigarette butt onto the ground and stomped it out with his foot. He then kicked it into the water.

Angelton crinkled his nose, "I suppose that love really is blind. You taught her all of this while you were married and now she's using it to protect herself. Nice move, Mary."

Jack and Wes stopped just short of meeting up with Marita. She continued to come toward them and stepped in between them.

"You're safe now, Marita. We're going to take care of you." Latimer gave her a cursory smile and turned on his heel to head back to the car.

Marita looked unsure. Jack placed an arm around her, "Come with me beautiful lady and I'll make sure no one ever bothers you again."

Onassis smirked when he saw Robert Kennedy enter his office. The secretary had announced Kennedy, but Aristotle couldn't believe he'd really have the balls to come.

"This must be a rare occasion for you to come to me, Kennedy. To what do I owe the pleasure? I'm surprised you're not at the convention."

"It's in Atlantic City, a mere helicopter ride away. Johnson was getting on my nerves so I've taken a break."

Onassis offered Bobby a seat and then gestured to the decanters in front of him. "Help yourself to a drink."

"No thank you. I won't be here long enough to sit or have a drink." Kennedy strode over to the window and glanced out. "Great view."

Onassis joined him and waited.

"I know that Duvalier is bringing some uninvited 'guests' to your party. I'm willing to give you those tapes you've been wanting for so long in exchange for these 'guests'."

August 25, 1964

Lyndon Johnson stood at the podium at the Democratic National Convention in Atlantic City. He waited for the applause to die down. "I know you've all been waiting to hear who I've chosen for my running mate. I've the great pleasure of announcing that Senator Hubert Humphrey from Minnesota has agreed to be placed on the ticket as your next Vice President of the United States of America!"

The applause was deafening as the news spread like wildfire. Flash bulbs went off all over the room as the news crews gathered vital information for tomorrow's addition of the paper.

Robert Kennedy sat there numb. He knew that Johnson would not put him on the ticket, but still it stung. His speech wasn't for another two days and he made up his mind right there how he would handle this slap in the face by Johnson. He sucked in a deep breath and left the room with as much pride and dignity as he could manage.

Hoover and Tolson sat at the diner across the street from the capital in total silence. They'd both been shocked at what Earl Warren had revealed to them in his interview with them.

Finally, Clyde broke the silence, "I can't figure out what the angle is on Johnson. Why would he want the Warren Commission and particularly the official report to show one bullet? One shooter?"

Hoover stirred his iced tea as he added a spoonful of sugar, "There is only one reason. He was behind at least one, if not more of the shootings and he is covering his back. What is interesting to me is that the media and the White House have simply forgotten that Connelly was shot as well. He was actually shot first and that round came through the front windshield of the car. Is that why Johnson sat in the back?"

"It is curious." Tolson took a French fry and dipped it in some ketchup. "It's clear that there had to be at least two shooters. I also want to know how the assassins knew the route had changed. It was last minute. They had to be tipped off by someone."

"Yes and it is clear that 'someone' was Johnson or perhaps his right hand man, Walter Jenkins. There was military code found at the book depository and Jenkins is military to the core." Hoover took one of Clyde's fries.

"Of course the greater question is, was that actually Kennedy who was assassinated? According to the Attorney General, it was not."

"Robert would know his own brother," Clyde sipped his cola.

"This situation is a potential powder keg. Why hasn't Kennedy resurfaced and regained his place as President?" Hoover glanced out the window. "If he did, what would happen? I still need to talk to Robert Kennedy and find out the particulars, but I think we've nothing to worry about as far as JFK coming 'alive' again."

"It would be interesting though, to see what would happen if he did suddenly appear from beyond the grave. People might think he's the Messiah or even the anti-Christ."

Hoover laughed, "Clyde, your mind is why I love you. You think in such a pragmatic way."

Ethel got behind the wheel of the car. She started down the driveway and stopped at a small stand of trees. Mary slipped into the trunk of the car, which Ethel had unlatched before she had driven off. The trunk closed on her and Ethel began easing the car out of the driveway.

Ethel passed the guard at the end of the driveway, gave him a cheeky smile, and turned out into the street breathing a sigh of relief as the house became a blur in her rear view mirror.

Chapter 12

Robert Kennedy took the podium on the last day of the Democratic Convention. Before addressing the assembly, he simply introduced a short film he had made in honor of his brother, John F Kennedy. As the film ended, he stepped back up to the microphone. The delegates burst into applause that lasted for nearly twenty-two minutes. Kennedy stood there, fighting back tears as he waited for the uproar to die down. Finally, the last delegate had been seated.

"Thank you all so much. I'm truly humbled here today." Bobby waited for the short round of applause to die down. "As I stand here, the recipient of your respect for my brother, John F. Kennedy...." More applause erupted. Finally, everyone seemed to settle down to hear what he had to say. Towards the end of his speech he purposely looked at Johnson, and finished with a quote from Romeo and Juliet, 'When he shall die, take him and cut him out into the stars, and he shall make the face of heaven so fine that all the world will be in love with night and pay no worship to the garish sun.' Shakespeare was eloquent and apparently understood true hero worship, as I had for my brother. There was no finer man, in my opinion, than Jack Kennedy."

The applause was spontaneous and continued for five minutes. Robert sat down as the next film began on the history of the Democratic Convention. He was pleased with his brother's legacy and the manner in which he had ignored the snub from Johnson. *This isn't the end of our quarrel. I've got plans for you, Mr. President, and I don't think you'll like them.*

Alice handed Georgi a plate as he came into the large kitchen at the farm. He filled it buffet style, and sat down.

Alice filled the iced tea glasses and placed them on the table, "How are you settling in?"

"I'm getting there. It's a pleasant enough house." He smiled at her to soften the harsh sounding compliment.

"I bet you'll soon agree with its name, Happy House. Once you're all settled in you'll enjoy it more."

Georgi took a bite of his roast beef. "Delicious. We rarely got anything this tasty in the Soviet Union."

"Thank you." She did a mock curtsy and settled herself into her chair. "We're getting a new defector today. She should be arriving this afternoon."

"Really? Soviet?" Georgia asked with interest.

"Yes and gorgeous from the rumors I've heard. Careful, sir, or you may just lose your heart."

Onassis raised an eyebrow. "Really? You'd give me the tapes over a couple of pieces of Duvalier's fiction? I now wonder how valuable these 'guests' are."

Kennedy squirmed slightly, "Look, they're no one important to you, just a couple of agents that have gone missing for a while. Duvalier is trying to squeeze more cash out of you and thinks you'll find these two worth the exchange."

"You know what? I think I'll see what old Papa Doc has up his sleeve. Besides, you've probably hacked those tapes to pieces by now. I no longer care about their contents." Onassis smiled, "Thanks for coming, though."

Prince Rainier III of Monaco arrived at the East Hampton airport in his private jet just about the same time the acting King of Saudi Arabia, Prince Faisal Saud, touched down. Prince Faisal's plane was taxied past Prince Rainier's in an effort to keep the monarchy in their correct place.

As Prince Faisal left his plane and entered the private limo awaiting him, the local uppity ups stared in amazement. Once the acting king was safely on his way, the private jet of the prince was allowed to taxi to a stop where the king's jet had just left.

Behind them came the private jet of Frank Sinatra with the Gabor sisters in tow.

"Oh my! Can you believe that there are two royals going to the Onassis party tonight?" Ava turned to Zsa-Zsa and Frank with glistening approval in her eyes.

"Maybe we can find us some rich husbands, dah-lin'." Zsa-Zsa teased her sister as she prepared to exit the plane.

Frank laughed, "As if you need rich husbands. You're after the title. You don't fool me."

Several of the locals stood watching from the little chain link barrier that kept them separated from the celebrities arriving. They cheered as each guest appeared in sight.

One of the more beautiful young ladies waved frantically to Frank, "I'd be happy to accompany you, Mr. Sinatra."

He smiled and answered back, "No thanks, but maybe I'll call you later."

He sent his driver to go get her phone number.

As the sisters stepped off the last step onto solid ground, the crowd went wild, begging for autographs. "I thought this was a snooty upper class neighborhood." Zsa-Zsa smirked as she waved to the crowd.

"It is, but we are royalty here." Frank gestured for them to get into the limo. "They'd rather say they met us than a king or prince because we carry more glamor than a foreign royal."

Norma rode in the back of the same van, the one with the bad shocks, that they had ridden in to the shack. Bill fell asleep as they bumped along the road. *How can he sleep with the ride being so rough?*

Norma allowed her mind to drift back to her stardom days. *It wasn't all great. Hoover tried to blackmail me and he wanted me to spy for him because he thought one of my lovers was a communist and I had 'communist ties.' I know I wasn't the only one he did that to. There was Frank Sinatra as well. He was pissed!*

I wonder how they're all doing. I know Hollywood has gone on without me, but some days I miss the glitz and glamour. I miss hiding out in hotels as Zelda Zonk. I miss dressing incognito to get around adoring fans in a pathetic attempt at being normal. I miss. . . .

They had come to a sudden stop and she heard shouting. Bill was fully awake. He gave her a nod. She quickly slipped out of the ropes that were tied around her wrists and ankles.

Bill was at the back door, opening it as she joined him. In one quick leap they were free of the van. Bill closed the door softly behind him as the van moved on down the street.

"Jenkins, let the First Lady know I'll meet her at the party. I'll change here at the office." LBJ waited for a response.

"I'll escort her, sir."

"Very good. I'll see you tonight, Jenkins."

Papa Doc Duvalier waited in the servant's quarters at the Onassis home for the van to arrive carrying his hostages. He saw them pulling up the drive through the window and headed out to meet his men.

The van pulled to a stop under the covered awning back of the servant's entrance as Papa Doc strode confidently to open the back doors. He caught hold of the latch and pulled the door ajar. He stared blankly at the empty van.

By this time the driver had left his seat and joined Duvalier at the back of the van. "Where the hell is fucking Marilyn?" Papa Doc leveled a fierce look at the driver.

"They were both tied up when we left. There were here. They should be here." He stammered to a stop as Duvalier punched him viciously in the mouth. The blow knocked him backwards into a pillar.

"Find them, you fucking idiot, or I'll kill you myself."

Onassis rounded the corner of the house in time to see the van speed away. Duvalier was spewing colorful language and was redder than the roses he stood next to. "What is all of this commotion?" Ari demanded. "I've got guests arriving and this is unacceptable."

Papa Doc took a huge breath and exhaled slowly. As his color began to return to a normal hue, he slumped into a folding chair that had been set there for the watch man for today's party.

"I had a surprise for you but she escaped." Defeated Duvalier just sat there looking for all the world like a two-year-old who had lost his favorite blankie.

"I had heard there were to be a few uninvited guests tonight. I don't suppose you'd let me in on who they are?

Or were?" Aristotle leaned down into Papa Doc's face, "After all, you are making a scene in my house and I do have a right to know the answer."

"It was Marilyn Monroe and a Soviet agent."

"The Marilyn Monroe? Are you mad? She's been dead for what, two years now?"

"No, she has NOT! Everyone thinks she's dead but she's still alive and I know it. John Kennedy is alive too and I am going to prove it."

"Duvalier, you really should go back to Haiti and rest yourself before all these fits of hysteria prove you're completely insane. I'm sure your people miss you. I'll tell everyone you're ill and extend your apologies." Onassis stood up.

Papa Doc stood with him, "I'm not ill. I'm furious. She's escaped. I've held her in my control for weeks. I should have summoned you to Canada to Barrier Lake, then you would have seen her."

"I can't see someone who is dead. Now go home. I want nothing further to do with a madman. You won't receive any more money from me." Onassis hailed his limo driver and watched while Duvalier was manhandled into the car.

"I don't ever want to see you again. If I do see you it'll be because we're celebrating your funeral." Onassis closed the door, nodded to the driver, and walked away as Papa Doc's fate was sealed.

Ethel pulled over to the side of the road and opened the trunk. Mary silently slipped out and into the backseat. Ethel resumed the driver's seat, checked the rear view mirror, and pulled back onto the road.

"So while we've got a little time to kill, let's chat." Ethel smiled in the mirror as Mary lay on the back seat.

"Chat? My life is in danger and you want to talk about what? Fashion? Weather?" Mary flipped onto her back and stuck her knees up.

"No actually I wanted to ask you why you decided to add Jack Lancer to your diary?"

"He's a crucial person in my life and I wanted to remember him. I was crushed by his assassination. You know I did my own investigation. The official one bullet equals one shooter didn't sit well with me.

"Cord kept notes for the CIA as well. I read his notes and added a few of my own. A spy should never show his wife the tricks of the trade." She chuckled at the memory.

"Honey, it's a good thing that diary is no longer in your possession. I just hope that you aren't writing anything else in a new diary." Ethel made a left hand turn and merged onto the freeway.

"Oh, I've been writing it down, old habits you know, but then I burn it to ashes in an old soup can. Once there is nothing left but ash, I dump the contents in the commode and have a brief ceremonial mourning service for them."

Ethel laughed at that, "Do you really?"

"No, but it sure sounded good. Cord said I was too honest and everyone knew when I was lying. Apparently, I've gotten better at it." Mary laughed as well.

"Just make sure you aren't leaving a paper trail." Ethel teased.

"Don't worry I've learned my lesson. I'm not even sure that this car isn't bugged."

Ethel looked around the car nervously, and in a hushed whisper she said, "Neither am I."

Maria Callas glided over to Ari, "Darling, why are you looking so out of sorts? It's a lovely afternoon and we're going to have such fun tonight." Maria laid a kiss directly on his surrendering lips.

"I'm sorry kitten, I assure you that the nasty bit of business is taken care of and all I want to do is focus my attention on your loveliness."

He placed an arm around her waist and walked with her back inside the house.

"Where am I staying, darling?" Maria whispered in his ear as the butler had another butler carry her luggage up the stairs.

"Alas, my children are here and it would not be right for you to share my room. I've placed you in the guest room directly across from mine. Not to worry. I know exactly where to find you."

Chapter 13

Bobby Kennedy sat at the diner stirring his iced tea with a spoon while Rex Stansel ordered his lunch. The waitress left and Bobby put the spoon on the table with a loud clunk.

"Here's where we are. Norma and Bill are still missing. They apparently left the van before it arrived at the mansion Onassis rented for this weekend. I have no idea where they are, but Kenny spoke to our mole inside the Onassis house who said there was a huge commotion from the servant's entrance and Duvalier was thrown off the property for making wild accusations about Marilyn Monroe being alive and slapping the van driver."

"Oh, wow! That throws a kink into our plans." Stansel leaned closer to Bobby, "What's the plan now?"

The waitress returned with Stansel's cola and a place setting. They waited until she was out of earshot.

"The plan is for you to fucking find out where they are and get them somewhere safe. That's the PLAN!" Bobby whispered fiercely. Stansel gulped down his soda, wrapped his newly arrived tuna sandwich in a napkin, and fled before Bobby could say another word.

Patricia Kennedy opened the back door of her home in D.C., and Ethel and Mary came in as Pat pushed the big boxer backward, "Down Brutus!"

As the ladies came into the kitchen, Pat managed to get the dog into his kennel and shut the door. She turned and gave Ethel a huge hug. "It's so good to see you!"

"It's good to see you too. It's been too long. There's just so much going on for both of us." Ethel stepped away from Pat, "You remember Mary Meyer?"

"Of course. Welcome to my home. I've had the maid make up a room in the guest wing. I'll try to keep the children quiet so you can rest and regroup." Pat patted Mary's shoulder, "Would you like something to drink? Tea? Vodka?"

They all laughed and sat down around the kitchen table as the maid prepared some martinis.

"I'm so grateful to be staying here. I hope you won't be too inconvenienced." Mary gave an unsure smile. "I'm also without any personal items, including clothes."

Pat laughed, "No reason to worry on that front, I've got more clothes than I can wear in three years. You can take your pick. I don't know if I'll be able to help in the shoe department though. What size are you?"

Mary grimaced, "I'm a size 7 ½. But I can squeeze into a 7 if I have to."

"I like you! We'll have fun together." Pat smiled and sipped her martini.

Ethel watched the two women, "So, any news on Peter?"

"No. I'm still trying to decide what to do. He wants to work it out, but I'm not so sure. Distance just makes me want to get a divorce, but New York is not happy to give us one. I may have to research another place to file for divorce. I hear Ohio is pretty liberal and will be fair to both parties."

"Oh Pat, I'm sorry it's not going to work out." Ethel stood up when Pat did.

"Okay, enough about me. Let's get Mary to her room and settled. I've already put a few things in there that you may want. Of course, you have your own bathroom included in the suite."

"Thank you so much." Mary followed Pat up the stairs with Ethel trailing behind.

"What about work?" Pat asked her.

"I sent a note around that I'm not feeling well and don't know when I'll return."

Bill looked around as Norma clung to his hand. "Where are we, Bill?"

"I'm not sure but since the van was going east, we'll be heading in the opposite direction. Let's look for a store or somewhere we can make a call."

They began walking. Norma's boots were slapping on the pavement with every step. "I'll be so happy to get rid of these stupid boots, and clothes and underthings. I'm just gross."

They walked for a mile or so noticing the gorgeous scenery. "I think we may be in the Hamptons." Bill noted as they walked along the straight road. "If that's the case, no one will pick up hitch hikers here. Too snooty." Bill placed his finger on the tip of his nose and pushed it upward.

Norma laughed. "Hey, there's a diner up there. I'm sure we can get them to let us borrow the phone."

"Are you sure? It is long distance." Bill looked doubtful.

"I'm sure. I just won't tell them." Norma smiled, "Don't underestimate me, my Bill. I'll handle this."

Hoover left another message for Bobby, "Please tell Mr. Kennedy that I'm tired of being ignored and demand a meeting with him."

"Is there a specific message I can give him?"

"Yes. Tell him that I have important information about what that bastard Onassis is up to with McIntyre and his dirty business techniques. He's trying to get docks in the U.S. for his ships. But of course, if the Attorney General is out of reach, I'll just have to hope the world doesn't go to hell before he gets back to me."

"Yes, sir. I'll give him the message."

Walter Jenkins finished putting together a quick list of what was working in the Vietnam conflict to aid in the Golden Triangle. With Onassis' party there wasn't time to discuss the list with Johnson so he placed it in a folder marked 'memos' and left it for LBJ.

The list was short but promising:

1) The advisers (aka troops) had been moved into Vietnam.

2) The two nuclear submarines had been ordered and there was plenty of money to be siphoned off the contract for all of them.

3) McIntyre is attending Onassis party. He will try to get him on board for the shipping angle.

Things weren't going as great as he'd like, but Jenkins was thrilled to have some positive news to report to the President.

Jack Lancer and Agent Wes Latimer had successfully taken Marita to the safe house where Georgie was currently living. The two men were driving back to D.C. from the farmhouse in Lake Jackson, Virginia.

"Well, that is one chore we managed to get done right. She'll be safe now and no one will ever find her." Lancer sat back and lit a cigarette.

Latimer just continued driving without comment.

"What do you know about the uprising in the Soviet Union?" Jack asked to pass the time.

"The agency's official stance is, of course, we don't know. My knowledge is Castro wants to oust the Premier because he will no longer press the button for a nuclear war. Apparently John Kennedy made him understand that if he sent nukes our way we would turn around and send them his way just as fast. Then both of our nations would be smoldering bits of marshmallows."

Jack smirked, "He was a smart man."

Latimer ignored his statement, "So, Castro is doing his best to stir up the dissidents to get Khrushchev tossed out. I doubt he'll live very long after he's outed. They generally meet with an accident."

"Yes, all we do is spy on one another and plot to kill the commander in chief. I wonder what the world would be like if we trusted each other?"

Latimer turned on his blinker and glanced at Jack as he slowed to make the turn. "We'd be like we were in the fifties where we were getting run over by all the world leaders because we were too gullible to understand they would lie to us."

Pat and Ethel watched Mary for a moment. She was very quiet and looked sad.

"I just have to tell somebody." Mary finally blurted out.

"Well, tell us!" Ethel leaned forward. Pat settled herself on the end of the bed as the three ladies got a bit cozier.

"I've been dying to share this but it was too dangerous. Now that I've told Ethel about my investigation of John's assassination I feel I should tell a little more about what I found out."

Pat waited but Ethel seemed antsy, "Do tell us! I have to get home and get ready for that damn party tonight with Jackie and Onassis."

"That's exactly who I wanted to tell you about. I actually overheard Jacquelyn Kennedy trying to seduce some guy into killing JFK at a party. She was pretty hammered but she was very sincerely offering him 'benefits' if he could arrange the death of her annoying husband."

Lady Bird was putting the finishing touches on her hair when she was interrupted by the maid, "Mr. Jenkins is here to escort you to the party, Mrs. Johnson."

The maid tittered behind her hand as she withdrew from the room. Outright laughter could be heard as the door closed.

Lady Bird shrugged and pulled on the matching gloves, grabbed the thin shawl and her evening bag, took one last satisfied look at her image in the mirror, and headed out to meet Walter Jenkins.

Bill and Norma entered the diner and asked to borrow the phone. Norma dialed Bobby's house number but only the maid answered. Bill then called the agency to inform them of where they were and what had happened. Once he hung up, they took a corner booth and asked for some menus. Bill kept searching the parking lot and watching the cars that went past out on the highway.

The waitress, though wary of how the two looked, brought them hot coffee and took their order. She removed the menus and Norma sat back with a sigh. "I finally feel safe."

Bill smiled at her, "You are safe."

"Maria Callas told me that it was Aristotle Onassis who wanted me dead. He ordered the hit and Dr. Greenson, my own shrink, came in and took care of me once Sam Giancana and his goon couldn't finish the job. What they didn't realize was the woman in my bed wasn't me. Bobby had come and rescued me by that point along with Peter." Norma allowed the tears to flow for a moment. She wiped them away with the cheap napkin.

"It must have been horrible for you." Bill leaned forward and touched her hand across the table.

"I was pretty beat up, kind of like now, only then I had a broken arm too, and lots of bruises. It was several days before I even knew what had happened for certain. Imagine being told that you are dead and must find a new life. I missed *my life.*"

"I can't even fathom it." Bill kissed her hand with gentleness.

"Where is my dog, Maf, that's short for Mafia? What happened to my estate? I mean there are still lots of questions I have been asking that no one ever answers for me."

The mansion was filling up with house guests and Ari was busy, so busy that he neglected to see Cary Grant come in. They were escorted up to their rooms as Ari dealt with the issues of having a large house party and ball in the same weekend.

The weekend was shaping up to be great as his guests gushed over the grounds, as well as the in ground swimming pool facing the ocean. Everyone was relaxing as the waiters circulated with trays of hors d'oeuvres and alcohol while the orchestra he had hired played softly.

Ari was a superb host and he knew how to make the most of his powerful presence. He turned to find Lee

Radziwill standing near his elbow. He kissed her on the cheek and took her hands in his. "Lee, dear one, it is so great that you were able to come."

She smiled at him, then leaned forward to give him a kiss. "It's my pleasure. So, my dear Ari, where am I staying for the weekend?"

"My children are here, so alas, you must reside in a guest room. But don't worry, I know exactly where to find you."

Chapter 14

Bobby and Ethel sat in the limo heading to the Hamptons from the private airport. Ethel was stiff and annoyed while Bobby was thoughtful and quiet.

They pulled up to the mansion without a word to one another and were greeted by a resplendent Jackie. She was dressed in a skin tight, gold lame gown that accented all of her curves. Her hands and arms were gloved in black elbow length silk. Her hair shimmered in the glow of the lit lamps along the path. In short, she was stunning.

The driver came around to open the door of the limo. As Bobby put his feet on the ground, Jackie came forward. "It's so good of you to come, Bob." She threw her arms around his neck as soon as he stood up straight. "Ethel." Jackie nodded in her direction and continued to hug Bobby.

"We're happy to show family support. You're a goddess in that dress." Bobby managed. Jackie finally untangled herself from him, smiled her acknowledgment and turned toward the front door, "Come and take a look at the dress Lady Bird is wearing, you'll just love it."

She grabbed Bobby's hand and led him toward the house. As they stepped up onto the lighted sidewalk Bobby spotted Christian Cafarakis motioning to him. He gave a slight nod and continued up the walk with Jackie and Ethel.

The guests were milling around inside the mansion, drinking and chatting happily amongst themselves. Aristotle greeted each as they entered and were announced.

He did a double take when Walter Jenkins was announced with Lady Bird Johnson. As the guests looked up to acknowledge the First Lady, there was a collective gasp in the room. Jenkins turned bright red and was doing his best to remain by her side.

Dressed in a gown that could only be described as an extremely large pineapple, Lady Bird smiled and came into the room to greet Onassis, the tips of her grass green shoes gleamed as she came down the few steps.

"What a delightful crowd you have here. I'm so looking forward to this evening." As she spoke, the green feathers protruding from her rather small round hat, bounced back and forth. Lady Bird removed the matching shawl and revealed thin shoulders in need of tanning. The spaghetti straps on her gown were made of gold lame and sparkled in the light of the chandeliers, while the cut of the gown revealed several overlapping layers of flouncy netting in yellow, brown, and green. The gown seemed to have a life of its own as Lady Bird moved in short flittering movements.

"It is my honor to have you here," Onassis finally found his voice. "What an unusual ensemble you're wearing."

Lady Bird smiled at the *compliment*. "Thank you. I hope I can surprise Lyndon, he's been a little too distracted lately." Lady Bird twirled around once for him and he smiled appreciatively.

"Oh, I'm certain it'll be a surprise." Onassis barely contained a snicker as a waiter stopped to offer them a drink from his tray. "Please, take a drink and make yourself comfortable. The President has already arrived."

"Thank you." Lady Bird smiled and wandered away in search of her husband.

Jenkins had escaped the very second that Lady Bird started talking with Onassis. He found the nearest waiter and gulped down a glass of champagne. He reached out for another when he noticed Lyndon hiding in the corner.

"Jenkins." He waved over his friend and confidante.

Reluctantly, Jenkins went over to the darkened corner and faced Johnson.

"Why the hell did you let her come wearing that get up?" The President whispered.

"Look, you just said to pick her up; you didn't say I had to approve of her outfit."

"Generally, I never have to worry about how she dresses. She's so, well, conservative, but this, this is outrageous. Does she think she's a sixteen-year-old girl at her first dance?"

"Really, sir, I couldn't say what she thinks other than she wanted you to find her attractive and you've been neglecting her of late." Jenkins shrugged.

"Excuse me for a moment, ladies." Bobby turned back to the front door. "I need to speak with one of the secret service men outside. I'll just be a moment if you'd wait for me."

Bobby kissed Ethel and she nodded her agreement. "I'll be right back, I promise."

Ethel handed her wrap to the maid and smiled at Jackie.

Bobby left the women and headed back down the steps. Christian was still standing in the dimly lit garden, well away from the cars arriving. He watched Bobby approach and moved into a small alcove of trees.

Christian began speaking before Kennedy even fully reached him, "Stansel received a call from Walton. He's on the way to pick them up now. They're safe for the moment in a diner. Stansel is taking several men with him just to make sure there is no trouble. No one knows where Duvalier is at the moment."

Bobby nodded. "Thanks. That's a relief."

"I've got to get back. If I'm caught, Onassis will kill me."

"Go." They both turned and walked away in opposite directions.

Lady Bird finally spotted her husband in an obscure corner with Walter. She grabbed a couple of drinks from the passing waiter and headed for him.

Lyndon noticed her approach and his face turned beet red. He waited for her to get close, took her arm, and dragged her behind a large potted palm.

Lady Bird was so startled she nearly dropped the drinks. She handed one to her husband with a puzzled look.

"What the devil are you wearing? You look ridiculous in that get up." Lyndon whispered fiercely.

Her tears sprung to the surface too quickly for her to suppress them. "What?" she managed in a faint whisper.

"Do you think you're some teenager trying to attract a man at the senior prom? Good lord woman, you're well over fifty. You should know better." He continued despite her tears. "Whatever possessed you to be such an idiot?"

She gulped and took a hankie out of her purse. She dabbed her eyes, wiped her nose, and stood up taller. "If you weren't ignoring me all the time I wouldn't have chosen this outfit to make you take notice. I'm your wife, Lyndon. I demand your attention. I have stood by you through the years, made you a millionaire, and put up with your twenty-year-long affair, but I will not be ignored or treated with disrespect any longer."

The vehemence in which she had spoken kept him silent for a moment too long. She took that cue and ran with it, "You will now escort me for the rest of the evening. You will not leave my side, cause me any embarrassment or say anything hateful, rude, or even remotely unloving. You owe me that much or I swear I will ruin you. After all, your lover and I both know your deep dark secrets." She leaned in to whisper in his ear, "**You** killed JFK."

Norma ate her hamburger with gusto, "I'm so glad to eat something tasty! Please pass the ketchup."

Bill handed it to her and she poured a good bit onto the plate and began dunking the French fries in it. Bill kept a watchful eye out the window and noticed a van pull up across the street.

He continued eating, and watched as three men got out of the vehicle. They approached a lone man standing in the darkened recess of an alleyway. The stores were all closed for the night and the sight was more than a little unusual.

Bill smiled at Norma, "Just keep looking at me. There are four men across the street who aren't looking very friendly at this moment. Stansel should be here soon but we need a plan in case he's a bit later than we'd like him to be."

Norma listened to him and continued to eat her fries. She smiled and nodded like he'd said something great and just kept acting normal.

"I'll need you to go to the back, through the kitchen, and out into the alley if they come in the front door. I doubt they will and they may even split up. It looks like Duvalier's men and maybe even Duvalier himself."

She took a drink of her soda. "Okay. Then what?"

"Then you will hide against the nearest wall and dumpster. I'll expect you to fight, just like I've showed you. You have the skills. You just need to take a deep breath and attack first."

"First?" Norma continued working on her burger.

"Yes. It gives you the upper hand. They won't be expecting it. Once you get a man down, run like hell. Try to find somewhere that has a crowd of people you can blend into."

"You know we're in the Hamptons, right? This is the biggest crowd you'll see tonight." Norma looked around at the one other couple who had just gotten up to pay their check. "They're leaving. That'll make us alone in here."

"Sitting ducks. Pray that Stansel and the rest of the cavalry arrive in time." Bill finished his meal and pushed his plate away just as two black cars pulled into the parking lot. "It looks like the show is about to begin. Are you ready, my love?"

J. Edgar sat next to Clyde on the bed. Clyde was shaking his head at the polish color choice Hoover had placed on his toenails. "It's not gaudy enough. I just don't feel like it suits me."

"What did you want? I only brought the pale pink and the lavender. I didn't want to alert anyone at the drug store.

"Yes, but you know I like bright colors with flamboyance. I need to feel like a woman."

"We have to be careful," Edgar ran his fingers along the length of Clyde's leg.

"I know we do. Surely we can arrange to leave a few things here with the Bell man. It's so hard to pack away our 'play things'. Someone is always watching.

"Speaking of that, what did you find out about Roselli? Did any of those bugs we planted yield the information we need to nab him?"

Tolson shook his head, "Not so far, but I really don't want to talk about two bit hoods right now. Kiss me."

Bobby returned to the ladies, who were still awaiting him in the long foyer. Ethel spotted him and rushed to his side. She took his hand and led him back to Jackie, "Do we have to stay long? I'd like to get back to the hotel and spend some alone time with you."

Bobby smiled, "Not long at all. In fact, I should be receiving an important message in about thirty minutes and that'll get us out of here."

Jackie joined them and they were announced to Ari. As they went into the ballroom, Bobby leaned down to Jackie, "I'll not play nice with that son-of-a-bitch. He's an ass."

"Be nice for me," Jackie pouted up at him with adoring eyes.

"Not even for you. Tonight I'm spoiling for a fight." Bobby stopped in front of Onassis' outstretched hand. "Onassis."

"Kennedy." Ari dropped his hand when he realized Kennedy wasn't going to shake it, and turned to Ethel, "Mrs. Kennedy, it's a pleasure to have you here at my party. Thank you for coming."

Bill watched as Stansel and several other agents began pouring out of the cars. The three thugs across the street returned to the vehicle and drove off down the street but turned into the alley behind the diner, leaving Papa Doc standing in the dark.

"I think the bad guys are coming in from the back. Stansel is here." Bill nodded to Norma. "You head out front and I'll get the men."

Norma went through the glass door and into one of the cars. She watched as Bill motioned the agents into the diner and through to the kitchen. Bill followed them into the back.

After about thirty seconds the cook and waitress came out into the eating area and left through the front door. As they were walking, the cook thumbed to his boss at the register, "Get out."

The startled manager looked up just as one of the agents burst into the dining room punching a large masked man in the face. The two scuffled for several moments before the agent pulled his gun. The manager ran out of the diner just as the gun exploded into the head of the masked man.

Kenny O'Donnell had heard from Stansel via car phone that they had arrived to meet Norma and Walton. He then hung up and called the Onassis party to let Bobby know they were safe.

Bobby followed the maid to the phone, "Kennedy."

"Stansel picked them up. There's a good fight going on right now to catch the kidnappers. What do you want done with survivors?"

"There's an abandoned police station in the Hampton Beach area, near the old bandstand. I'll be there tomorrow to discuss what happens with whoever you arrest. Keep this under wraps for now. I don't want this to go public."

Onassis came up behind Jackie and put his arms around her. He kissed her neck as she leaned back into him. "I approve of your dress, my dear. It leaves little to the imagination. Of course, I'm well aware of the beautiful package wrapped so deliciously in that gold gown." He kissed her neck again and turned her around to face him.

"You know that I want nothing more than to marry you. Why do you persist in making me wait?"

Jackie finally spoke, "I don't want to upset my children by adding a new daddy to their world too soon. It won't be much longer. We'll get all moved in and settled in the next few months here in New York. Things will smooth out. You'll see the children, and they will get accustomed to you." She pressed her breasts against his chest and kissed his lips.

He groaned and tried to pull her closer but she slipped out of his arms with a soft giggle, "You've guests that need to be attended to. This can wait until later."

Chapter 15

Norma watched the employees flee from the diner as she opened the car door. They hid behind the cars where a few of the agents were watching out for Norma. After the masked man was shot in the diner, another agent rounded the corner chasing a man on foot. She jumped out of the car and spotted a large tree branch lying on the ground near the sidewalk She reached down and grabbed it, and swung with all her might, just as the man came running at her. He flew into the plate glass window and landed with a sickening thud inside the diner on top of a small table. The chairs scattered every which way when his limp body came to rest on the floor as the table collapsed.

Bobby Kennedy greeted McIntyre as he was heading back to Ethel. "What are you doing here?" Bobby asked surprised, extending his hand to shake Thomas' hand.

"Just a little pleasure and some business. You know how we politicians are." McIntyre smiled blandly.

"Yes, I do. You're not here to try to make a deal with Onassis about some ships or something are you?" Bobby took out his cigarette case and opened it.

"Anything is possible. You know I've got to look for revenue, wherever it may be, for my state." McIntyre walked away as Bobby lit the cigarette and blew out the first satisfying puff.

Pat and Mary sat watching Ed Sullivan, eating pizza and drinking wine. They had settled in for the night and Brutus was curled up beside Pat with his big head on her house shoes.

Mary waited for a commercial, "Do you think that Jackie knew the bullets weren't for her? Did she know he was going to be assassinated?"

"She is a cold bitch. I have never liked her. She has asked Joe for money since the day she agreed to marry John. We embraced her as family because we had to, but not because we wanted to. Frankly, I'm happy she's moving away from D.C. and getting a new start." Pat finished her pizza and gave the crust to Brutus. He eagerly gulped it down and wagged his stub at her in appreciation.

"While I was investigating John's death, it occurred to me that she didn't duck and hide like any normal person would. Shock or no, your first instinct would be to protect yourself. I just don't get it." Mary shook her head and handed Brutus a piece of pepperoni.

"We've all had that very same question. I'd love to know the answer."

"The answer has to be she knew it was coming and she wasn't surprised." Mary took a sip of her drink, "After all, she was tired of him. There was no love lost between the two of them. The only thing Jacquelyn Kennedy was concerned about was the sympathy she could wrangle out of the American people, for the grief stricken widow, saddened by the loss of her imaginary Camelot. What a load of shit!"

While the other agents were engaged in the fighting, Bill slipped outside and into the alleyway. He jogged down the alley to the street, noticed the brightly lit street lamp, and continued down the next block to the other end. The light was burned out and he quickly crossed the street where Papa Doc was hiding.

He snuck quietly toward Papa Doc but stopped, mesmerized as Norma took out one of the goons with a tree limb. He smiled and continued on his way down the street.

He had Papa Doc cornered before the man knew what hit him. Bill yelled out for help and Stansel leapt to his side. With barely a struggle they had taken Papa Doc into custody. Norma ran over to them and kicked the Haitian prince in the nuts. He screamed in pain and doubled over. She then karate chopped him on the back of the neck sending him sprawling to the ground. She shook her hand out in front of her because it was still stinging from the blow and smiled at Bill. "Thanks for the lessons in self-defense."

She turned and sauntered back across the street.

Bobby had gone to find Ethel a non-alcoholic drink when Frank Sinatra sidled up to him, "Great speech at the convention."

"Thank you so much." Bobby smiled, as he approached the bar. "I'm sure Jack would have been touched."

"Oh," Sinatra swirled the drink in his hand, "wasn't he there? I really thought he'd like to see such a moving tribute and the way folks reacted to him."

"No, he was otherwise engaged." Bobby ordered Ethel a Shirley Temple and waited for the bartender to make it.

"I'm glad you're running for Senate. I think you'll be excellent. I just wanted to let you know how much I liked the video and speech you gave. You've a real talent for getting people to listen to you. I bet you'll be President someday." Sinatra held out his hand, "I'll vote for you."

Bobby shook his hand, "Thanks. I appreciate your support."

Jackie excused herself and went upstairs to check on the children. She opened the door to the playroom. Caroline and John-John sat in the middle of the room with Christian playing with Lincoln Logs. Christina and Alexander were in the corner watching television.

"Mama," Caroline came over and hugged her mother's legs. "Look what we're building."

Jackie smiled at her daughter and ruffled her hair. Caroline took her mother's hand and led her to where the guys were engrossed in their building.

"It's a shipping dock, with ships." Caroline explained.

"I see that." Jackie leaned down for a closer look. The little toy battle ships were lined up close to a dock built with flat Lincoln Logs, while the main building held other little boats constructed out of paper.

"Very good!" John-John glanced up and she patted his head. "It's about time for you two to go to bed. I just came up to say good night."

They dutifully hugged and kissed her. "I'll make sure they go to bed soon, Mrs. Kennedy." Christian placed another Lincoln Log on the nearly complete building. "We're almost done here anyway."

"Thank you." Jackie turned to leave as Christina approached her. She made it to the door of the playroom before the child spoke.

"Why did you have to come here? You're the worst kind of person." Christina burst out.

"Well, really! Where do you get off talking to me like that?" Jackie was appalled.

"You're not my mother and you're only after the power and money my dad has. You may fool him with your little act, but I know you're just a bitchy ice queen out for more money, more status, and more gifts."

Jacquelyn reached up to slap her pert little face, thought better of it, and stormed out of the room. She heard Christina laughing on the other side of the slammed door.

Papa Doc Duvalier was roughly pulled to his feet. "You can't do this to me!"

Stansel nodded over to Bill Walton and he came close to Duvalier. "We are placing you in custody by orders of the Attorney General of the United States of America for suspicion of unlawfully detaining citizens of the U.S."

"You'll pay for this!" Duvalier broke his right arm free and raised a fist into the air.

"No sir, I doubt that. You're also being investigated for treason, unlawful entry into this country, and whatever else we can come up with. I doubt you'll see the light of day for many years to come." Stansel had him pushed into the back seat of a vehicle.

"You didn't cuff him." Walton observed.

"Can't. We don't have anything on him yet."

"Norma can testify that he came to visit us in the shack in Canada."

"Not our country and he wasn't transporting you. All we can hope to do is scare him to death and maybe we'll get some useful information about Onassis out of him."

Stansel headed to the other waiting car. "Come on. You two need to get some real rest, perhaps a shower and some decent clothes."

Norma held out her hand to Bill as they walked to the car. "Of course you have the right to cuff Duvalier. I know better than anyone that this agency does what it wants to whomever it wants. We make the rules, not follow them."

Stansel stopped walking and turned to Bill, "A lot has changed since you've been traipsing around the world with Ms. Baker. We'll talk about it in the morning."

Bill followed them to the car without another word.

Hoover was all dressed up in his favorite vamp outfit while Clyde was wearing a gorgeous dress from the roaring twenties. Hoover loved how the fringes moved when Clyde walked. Both wore long wigs with bangs and heavy foundation makeup. No one would have ever recognized them as the FBI's most powerful men. As they entered the Stork Club, Hoover stopped Clyde, "Isn't that Cole Porter heading in?"

Clyde held up a monocle to his eye, "It is. Who is he with?"

Hoover shook his head, "I don't know but I'd kill for those legs."

Bobby returned to the phone, "Kennedy, is everything taken care of?"

O'Donnell answered, "Yes. We have him in our possession. What do you want us to do with him?"

"Secure him in the location we already talked about, and keep him guarded until morning. I am needed here. There are many politicians I need to speak with and Duvalier will be more willing to cooperate with me after he's had an opportunity to calm down."

"What about Latimer? They have completed that mission and are ready for a new one."

"Have them come here, O'Donnell. We may need a little help persuading Duvalier to help us. Lancer is our man." Bobby hung up the phone.

He stood for a moment the beginning of a grin on his face. He shook his head and went back to the party.

Norma was settled in her bed. She was too wired to sleep. Bill had taken the room next to hers and she could hear him snoring through the wall. *Either these are super thin walls or I'll need earplugs if we ever do marry.*

She picked up the phone's receiver, waited a moment, and dialed the operator. She gave her the long distance number.

The phone rang several times before it was answered, "Hello?"

"Barbara? It's Norma. I'm safe!" Norma burst into pent up tears as she told her dear friend all about what had happened since they'd last seen each other.

Papa Doc was shown into a dimly lit cell in the basement. The lights were still off in the main building upstairs as the agents secured the door. There was a flurry of activity as they moved desks down near his cell and set up the guards at the end of the hallway. There was only one way in and one way out.

Duvalier watched as they silently got everything into place and discussed in whispered tones who would take the first shift as guards.

He sat on the cot with an exhausted thump. *What do you hope to gain from me, Kennedy? Don't you know* **I** *can control you? My magic is just as powerful here as in Haiti. Never fear, my hatred will conquer you.*

He began to chant and tap his foot in rhythm to his own music. After a couple of minutes, the agents had decided on the evening's routine. One of the guards came over to the cell and slammed his pistol butt against the metal door.

Papa Doc jumped off the bed, snapping out of his trance in one quick movement.

"No Noise! If I hear another sound from over here I will shoot you." The agent stood starring at Duvalier without blinking. The mighty Haitian prince sat down with a silent nod.

"Good. I have excellent hearing. It's why I got in the agency. Well, that and my precision shot. I doubt you'll want to test either."

Chapter 16

McIntyre was just getting settled near the pool when he spotted Onassis bearing down on him. He nodded toward Ari to show that he saw him.

"Onassis, splendid party! I'm enjoying myself immensely." McIntyre held out his hand. "It's a very clever way to get us to like you and your generosity."

Ari accepted McIntyre's hand with a hearty handshake, "Hopefully, everyone will like it without realizing the 'why's'. I'd like to talk business with you in the morning, say before breakfast? We could have a nice walk along the beach with the President."

"I'll be there. Although I doubt Lyndon will agree to meet at such an early hour." McIntyre blew a smoke ring from his lit cigarette.

"My thoughts exactly, but he'll know we're meeting. He'll believe he knows why but he won't know everything, now will he?"

"Shrewd. I've heard that about you."

"McIntyre, have you also heard that you don't want to cross me once an agreement or deal has been reached?" Onassis walked away without waiting for his answer.

Bobby and Ethel walked along the beach holding hands. They had taken off their shoes, socks or pantyhose, and walked along in the romantic moonlight.

"Bobby, I need you to know that Mary Meyer came to the house this morning."

Bobby stopped as he released her hand, "What? Why?"

"It's your fault. No one has been protecting her and she was nearly killed. She had nowhere to go and she was terrified."

"Sweet Mother of Jesus, where is she now? Not at our house! Please say she's not there." Bobby grabbed her hand again.

"She's not at the house and no one saw her aside from the maid and she doesn't know who she is. Mary did have to tell the secret service men outside our house who she was, but I bet you can contain that problem."

"How did you get her out, Ethel?"

"I snuck her. She jumped into the trunk of the car halfway down the driveway where that stand of trees is."

Bobby laughed, "I can picture it."

"She's at Pat's." Ethel kicked some sand with her toes.

"No, she can't stay there either. We need to get her moved. I'll have someone go get her and take her home. I promise she'll be guarded day and night. She has to continue her normal life." Bobby turned back toward the party.

"Why? Why does she 'have to'? Spill it."

"She's too involved with Jack and we need her to be normal or she'll blow the cover. He's in danger now as well. She has to act as though nothing is wrong. It can be a weekend at her girlfriend's but she's got to be back by Sunday night and go to work on Monday as usual. Jack doesn't need this right now, none of us do."

Jackie stood in Ari's room after the party. He was undressing her slowly and kissing her passionately as he did so. She moaned and leaned into his masculine strength. He finished unzipping the gown and helped her wriggle out of it. She stood there in her slip and stockings allowing him to take in her figure.

"Ari, darling, we must discuss Christina."

"Not now, woman." He had sat her gently on a nearby chair and began unrolling her stockings first, removing the garter on each slim thigh.

"But we must. She was very, very rude to me tonight. She even yelled at me that I'm not her mother and I needed to leave you alone." Jackie bent her face to his. "I won't tolerate being spoken to in such a manner by anyone."

"She's a kid. She misses her mother and doesn't know that her mother doesn't want her there. Please try to be patient. It'll work itself out."

"She's a horribly behaved young lady! She needs to be taught some manners. Adults always deserve respect!" Jackie stood up, knocking him back on his heels.

Onassis righted himself, and stood up with his Greek temper rising. "I don't believe you! What did she say that was sooo terrible?" He stormed over to the night stand and lit a cigarette.

"She said, and I quote, 'You're not my mother and you're only after the power and money my dad has. You may fool him with your little act but I know you're just a bitchy ice queen out for more money, more status, and more gifts'."

"Well, that isn't nice, but none of it is a lie. What she doesn't know is that we're using each other. I want you for your access to the American public and status you'd bring me and you want my money. I don't see what the fuss is about."

Jackie stood there, "The 'fuss' is she's rude, impertinent and hateful. I should not ever be spoken to like that whether she likes me or not!"

"She's allowed to speak freely. Isn't that a perk of your wonderful country? Home of free speech?"

"Seriously?" Jackie picked up her dress and garters, then stormed from the room leaving Ari standing with his mouth wide open.

Lyndon Johnson had taken Lady Bird back to their room at the mansion. It had been a long day and he was ready to forget everything she had done at the party. He was getting ready to retire for the night when a knock sounded at the door. He opened it to reveal McIntyre.

"What do you want?" The President stepped out of the room and closed the door softly behind him.

"Onassis wanted me to invite you to join us at five in the morning for a private chat. He thinks it would benefit us all."

"What's this all about?"

"He wants shipping docks in New Hampshire and I'm all for it. It would create plenty of revenue and jobs for my state."

"Well, that's not really anything new. I doubt that you'll ever be able to sell the idea to your constituents. Everyone hates Onassis and until he can find acceptance you'll be hard pressed to get support on the idea. It's already been shot down in Boston and New York City." The President turned the door knob.

"I'm just trying to say, I think I can win over the voters in my state." McIntyre persisted.

"Do whatever you like. I'm going to bed and I'll see you both at breakfast. This is a meeting that I definitely don't need to be at, not at five in the morning. One thing I know for sure, don't trust anything he says without a written, signed document. He's a shrewd businessman and he's slippery." Johnson opened the door and left McIntyre standing alone in the hall.

Jacquelyn Kennedy stormed past a startled McIntyre as a flustered Onassis followed suit. McIntyre blinked a couple of times as the feminine partially dressed woman left nothing to a man's imagination. McIntyre shrugged, turned back to his room, and kept his mouth shut.

Barbara hung up from Norma and called Gregory. He answered on the first ring, a habit most agents learn. "Morris."

"Gregory, it's Barbara," she blushed, "I'm sorry to call you like this but I thought you'd like to know that Norma is safe in the Hamptons."

"Of course, honey. I'm so glad that you called. Tell me all about it. I'm sure I'll get some sort of briefing about it but it's not really my case."

August 29, 1964

Jack Lancer sat next to Wes Latimer as they turned onto Main Street, East Hampton. He watched Latimer turn into the parking lot next to the old gazebo. They both appreciated the view of the water as they turned into the old precinct.

"Look." Latimer pointed at the signs being posted on the doors of the police station.

Lancer read, "Private function by order of the mayor."

They both laughed out loud as they pulled into a parking space next to a couple of black sedans.

Latimer was out of the car first and began talking to the agent posting the signs. "Of course the mayor has given no such order."

Stansel turned as he heard his partner's voice, "Latimer, good to have you here." He nodded to the sign, "Yes, but who would question the mayor?"

Lancer joined them and they all headed down into the basement. "We have to take the stairs. We're working on getting the power back on but right now we are just using the generator."

"No problem." Latimer headed down the flight of stairs.

"Who's the prisoner?" Latimer asked, "I was just told to report here and you'd fill me in."

"It's Duvalier. He's under some 'delusion' that Marilyn Monroe is alive and he has proof. He says she kicked him last night and are we all blind?"

"Oh yea, we're all blind. That's our girl Norma, but definitely not Marilyn Monroe." Lancer chuckled as they all agreed.

"Why is he here, really?" Latimer asked.

"Unofficially he's here at the invitation of Robert Kennedy. Apparently, he thinks Duvalier has some information about Onassis' involvement in his brother's death.

Cord Meyer sat sipping his coffee and reading the sports section of the newspaper in a crowded D.C. diner. He looked up as the bell jingled over the door announcing the comings and goings of patrons. He frowned as Jim Angelton headed straight towards him.

Jim sat down, "Cord." He nodded to the waitress as he motioned to the coffee mug in front of the man across the table from him.

"Jim. What are you doing here?"

The waitress nodded and headed to the back to get him a fresh cup.

"I'll be honest. I've been watching you for some time trying to see what you know about Mary."

"Honesty is refreshing in this business." Cord frowned at him, "Why would you think I know anything about her?"

"For exes, you two seem to have a pretty solid relationship." Jim smiled as the waitress handed him his coffee, "Thank you." He smiled and patted her butt as she walked off.

"She's come to see me a few times lately but I have no idea what she's been up to."

"Well, for one," Jim added creamer and sugar to his mug and stirred it with the metal spoon, "her diary is still MIA. We need to get that from her ASAP."

"Then what?" Cord tried to be causal about the question.

"Then, after it has been secured, she'll need to go." Jim sipped the still hot coffee.

"Is that really necessary?"

"Yes, she knows too much. All that investigation over JFK has put her on the hit list. The last thing the administration needs is a loner out there with sensitive information."

Cord shook his head, "I disagree. If she was going to say something about it she would have already done so. You don't need to worry about her."

"Maybe, maybe not, but we're not willing to wonder about her or what she might or might not do. It's up to you to get that diary or we'll think you've got something to hide as well."

Jim threw a couple of dollars on the table and got up. "You have one week."

Chapter 17

<u>August 30, 1964</u>

Norma and Bill had finished breakfast and were waiting out front for the car to come pick them up at the hotel.

"I'm thinking of retiring." Bill suddenly announced.

Norma watched him quizzically, "Really? To do what?"

Bill squinted his eyes for a moment, deep in thought, and took her hand, "I'd like to maybe buy a small place and have a life with you, if you'll have me."

She laughed softly, "Is that a proposal?"

He squeezed her hand, "It depends on what your answer would be."

"Well, how would you provide for us?" She turned to him suddenly serious.

"I should get a good hazard payout for this latest adventure. I'd like to find a sleepy little town where nothing much happens and the cost of living is small. We could get by on my pension if we could buy a house outright from the large sum I'll get for taking such good care of you in the wilderness." Bill took hold of her other hand. "I know it's not the limelight you're used to or the big fancy houses or cars you adore, but I promise I'll always be good to you and love you till my last breath."

Norma sighed and leaned in to kiss him. The car arrived and the driver honked furiously at them. They got up with reluctance.

"I'll await your answer, my love." Bill kissed her hand as he placed her into the back seat. He then jumped in the front to catch up with what had gone on during the night shift.

Jackie arrived in the dining room a few minutes after Lady Bird. Both women were in a bad mood. They scowled at each other as Jackie was seated by the attentive waiter.

"Onassis never spares any expense in impressing his guests, does he?" Lady Bird commented as her coffee was refilled by another waiter.

Jackie looked around, but there was no one else in the room the First Lady could be speaking to. "Are you seriously opening a conversation at this ungodly hour?"

Lady Bird bristled, "Yes, it seemed the civil thing to do."

"Don't bother." Jackie nodded to the waiter holding a coffee urn. He filled her cup and held the silver plate with cream and sugar on it for her to get her drink just right. She shook her head and he backed away.

"There is no need to be rude." Lady Bird stirred her coffee, "I know we don't like one another but rudeness should never be tolerated in public."

"We're not in public."

"We could be at any moment and you're making the situation a bit embarrassing." Lady Bird picked up a slice of toast and buttered it lightly.

"If you'd like embarrassing, I'll be happy to accommodate you. Tell your husband that I do appreciate him leaving me alone and would certainly hope that he will continue to behave himself. It's not good for him to be pawing me every time we're in a room together." Jackie leaned away from the table as a plate was sat in front of her. The morning boiled egg, one slice of toast and one piece of bacon called to her.

Lady Bird's spine stiffened as she thought about her response, "It would seem to be that a floosy like you would be used to such advancements toward her. After all, what you put out will be returned in spades."

Aristotle walked along the beach in bare feet with McIntyre struggling along in his tennis shoes. Ari stopped when they were a good distance from the mansion. "Congressman McIntyre, I hope you're having a nice visit. It's been a pleasure having you here."

McIntyre laughed, "You certainly know how to schmooze your guests. I've enjoyed seeing you throw around your wealth."

Onassis smiled, "Why not? I've got it and I'll never be able to spend it all. The thing is, I really would like to get my ships into the American ports but I seem to face problems with every turn."

"I'd love to help you with that. I've talked to the Governor of New Hampshire and he's amenable to allowing you to have shipping docks in any port you'd like. For a price."

"Just name it and I'll be happy to meet you at least halfway."

"What about the President? How will this deal affect him?" McIntyre strode beside a now moving Onassis.

"He's going to be thrilled." Aristotle smiled and held out his hand to Thomas McIntyre.

"Then with that blessing, let's move forward." Thomas grasped Onassis' hand and they shook on the deal.

Onassis nearly jumped with excitement. "This will be mutually beneficial."

Papa Doc watched the parade of people come up and down into the basement. He hadn't slept much during the night because the agents kept waking him up to see if he needed anything.

He yawned when the newest arrivals descended the staircase, but snapped to full attention once he realized it was Jack Lancer, a.k.a. John F Kennedy, who had entered the hallway near his cell.

Jack stood talking with the other agents while Papa Doc gawked. After a few moments, Lancer went back upstairs without ever fully looking at Duvalier.

Duvalier sat down on his cot with a thump, "What the hell is he doing here?" He murmured to no one. "I can't deal with this. I've been chasing him for so long and he just walks in here happy as you please?"

He placed a hand over his wildly thumping heart. He took a couple of deep breaths. Stansel walked over to his cell, "Would you like some breakfast?" He handed a sandwich through the bars and a small Styrofoam cup with orange juice in it.

Duvalier took it and returned to his cot, struggling to breathe normally.

"Hey, are you okay?" Stansel watched him.

"Fine. Just fucking fine."

Bobby finished tying his shoe lace as Ethel watched from the bed. "I hope I won't be too long honey, but it's that business from last night." He came over to the bed and kissed her.

"I understand. I'll have a nice long bath and when you get back we'll talk about how you're going to deal with Mary."

"Oh, no we won't. She came to you, so it's your problem." Bobby backed away from the bed and inched closer to the hotel door.

"But you didn't protect her so I think it's your problem." Ethel smiled up at him, "Besides, you're so good at this sort of thing."

Jack followed Latimer upstairs, "I need to run an errand. Can I borrow the car?"

Latimer turned to look at him, "What for?"

"I won't be long. I just need to do something."

Latimer shrugged and tossed him the car keys, "Why don't you wait until Bobby gets here?"

"He won't even miss me. I'll be back in a few hours." Jack pocketed the keys as he turned to study the big area map on the wall.

"What should I tell everyone?"

"Tell them I've gone for some decent coffee." Jack smiled and headed out the glass doors.

Onassis had reached his suite in the mansion. He opened the door to find Christina sitting on the love seat in his sitting room.

"Good morning! This is a surprise. What are you doing up so early?" Ari walked over to his daughter and kissed the top of her head.

She scowled, "I'm too old for that."

He backed up and sat down in the chair beside her. He waited.

She fidgeted a little and then blurted, "I heard through the servant's grapevine that you and your precious ice queen had a public squabble last night."

He raised a dark eyebrow.

"I think it is ridiculous that you were chasing her through the hall like some love sick puppy. I hate her, Daddy. Can't you find someone else to date?" Christina wiped a tear away.

"Oh bravo," Ari applauded. "A magnificent performance. I see you've been watching too many soap operas."

She sniffed and turned her full anger upon him, "She's just using you. She's a money-hungry, power-mad bitch and I hate her." Christina stood up and stomped her foot.

Ari stood up and struck her across the face. She reached up to cover the mark, but didn't move. "Let me tell you something. I will not tolerate insolence in anyone, even my own daughter. You will be nice to her and you will try to get along with Jacquelyn Kennedy. She is our ticket into American society and no one else can give us that."

"You don't love her," Christina nearly whispered.

"No, nor does she love me. She wants money and security, and I want acceptance and business in the states. We can both win here if you'll only behave. My naive child, it's all about how you play the game."

Cary Grant, Frank Sinatra, and the Gabor sisters came into the dining room just as Lady Bird was finishing her breakfast. They were laughing and discussing the latest Hollywood gossip.

Good morning," the First Lady interrupted the conversation. "It's a lovely day isn't it?"

"Lady Johnson," Cary Grant came over to her chair and took her hand in his, "It is indeed a glorious morning." He kissed the air above her hand and gave her that dazzling smile.

She melted at the attention, "I . . . I didn't mean to upset your discussion. Please do continue."

"Nonsense! It is rude of me not to have noticed such beautiful ladies when I walked in. Your radiance is beyond compare." He sat down beside her giving her his full attention.

Lady Bird's face turned a lovely shade of red as he ordered tea with a dab of milk in it. She turned back to her own empty cup of coffee and suddenly decided to stay.

The waiter had noticed she was staring at her cup and immediately filled it. "My apologies, my lady." He backed away and brought her the silver plate full of cream and sugar.

Frank and the Gabors had sat down opposite the company and were deep in their own conversation. Jackie sat there, utterly alone in the group. She sat there for a moment more and then got up, "Well, have a good day everyone." She smiled as she said it and waved at them as she left.

Of all the nerve! Have I suddenly become invisible? Jackie fumed as she controlled her pace and body language. No one even noticed that she'd left. *What the hell is wrong with everyone? Have I lost 'it'?*

As she headed out into the garden for a stroll and some thought she ran into Prince Rainier.

He bowed over her hand, "Good morning, Mrs. Kennedy."

"Good morning. I'm just heading out for a walk. Are you searching for breakfast?" She smiled as she gently pulled her hand from his.

"Yes, thank you."

"You'll find everyone in the dining room. The boiled eggs are done just right if you like that sort of thing." She turned to go out the French doors.

"Thank you." He gave a slight bow and left her.

Well, that's better. Jackie's ego had been repaired and she walked with a jaunty step out into the garden.

Norma and Bill arrived at the police station and were shown into the big conference room where all the off duty agents were gathering for the briefing. They were waiting for Robert Kennedy to arrive. Stansel had gone to pick him up and they were on their way back to the precinct.

Bill was greeted warmly by comrades who had been with him either at the park where he ran after Norma or had worked with him on other operations. Even though

Bill Walton had been in Russia, he was a well-respected agent.

Norma watched as he enthusiastically retold every detail to the mesmerized group of men. He pulled her over to them as she told her story.

"Ms. Baker, why do you think you were targeted by the kidnappers?" someone asked.

"While it is silly and flattering at the same time, I was mistaken for the deceased Marilyn Monroe. Can you just imagine anything so ridiculous?" Norma laughed at the thought.

"What did they want?"

"Duvalier has it in his mind that Marilyn Monroe is still alive and could be a valuable asset to him against some of the more powerful men in the world. For what gain I cannot understand. So I played along and acted like I was Ms. Monroe because he'd already threatened us." Norma shook her head, "He's crazy and he'll use voodoo magic on you if you give him half a chance. If he starts chanting or dancing stop him."

The guys nodded. They continued to ask her questions about the ordeal as Bill watched with a smile. *Oh yeah, my love has got this! They're buying every word she says.*

Chapter 18

Stansel pulled up under the awning at the hotel. Bobby saw him stop and headed out to meet him. He jumped in the front seat and Stansel signaled and took off toward the main road.

"I've finished with all of the tapes." Rex told him as he merged onto the highway.

"Is there anything worth reporting?" Bobby lit a cigarette as he watched Stansel.

"Actually, there was quite a bit." Stansel glanced at Kennedy.

"Give me a brief outline. It won't take long to get to the police station." Bobby blew out a lungful of smoke.

"Okay. She had been rehired by Fox to finish *Something's Gotta Give*. She'd been in talks with her attorney about starting her own production company. She knew about the numerous attempts on Castro's life because the President chose to share those details as pillow talk. He also shared the deal he'd made with Khrushchev to avoid nuclear war. She knew that Onassis was mad enough at her to kill her over her refusal to marry a prince in order to help Onassis gain the trust of the American public. She knew all about the

Golden Triangle and Johnson's part in it." Stansel took a breath as Bobby watched him intently, "Marilyn basically had enough information to bring down the entire Kennedy clan. What she had called the press conference for, was the way John had unceremoniously dumped her. Then he sent you to come and give her the bad news when she finally would be ignored no longer."

"Is that all?" Bobby sighed.

"Nearly, she mentioned to her attorney that if she died it would be murder. She wanted to have a good life, free of you Kennedys and free of the crap politics brought her."

Bobby nodded but kept his thoughts to himself.

After a few moments Stansel asked, "So did you know about all of this?"

"Most but not all. I did go talk to her earlier in the evening on the night she died. I tried to get her to cancel the press conference because as you said, she would ruin us. Teddy would never get into the Senate if she held that conference."

"Who sent the word to kill her? Joe? John? Was it you?" Stansel left the highway and turned into the precinct.

Jack pulled his black vest on over the white starched long sleeved shirt. He stood in line with a few others and waited until he got the nod from the chef.

"Go circulate in the garden with a tray of drinks from the bar."

Jack nodded and headed out of the kitchen into the vast hallway that would lead him to the den where the bar had been set up for the weekend. He grabbed his tray filled with champagne and orange juice then carefully followed the instructions out to the garden area.

A few couples were strolling and took glasses from his tray. He kept walking until he nearly ran into Jackie.

She was standing staring at a gorgeous rose bush in full bloom blocking the path.

He cleared his throat and she moved, "Oh, excuse me." She didn't look up from the rose she was inspecting.

"Jacks," he whispered as he placed his tray on a nearby park bench.

She jumped at the sound of his voice and turned in slow motion to face him. He smiled as she looked at him. After a few seconds she started to wobble on her feet. He reached out and took her elbow. Leading her to the bench he set her down with a gentleness that surprised him. "Jacks."

She finally found her voice, "John?"

"You know it's me." He stroked her arm in little caressing movements.

She jerked her arm away and slapped him full across the face, "How dare you show up here!" She stood up and grabbed his hand, pulling at him as she darted back down the path.

"What are you doing?" John asked as they nearly sprinted through the garden.

"I'm taking you to Ari." She stopped and turned back to face him, "I need him to see you so he'll understand I'm not crazy. Do you know how much trouble you've caused me?"

"I can't see anyone else, Jacks, I'm sorry."

"Oh yes you will. You owe me that much at least." Jackie continued to cling to his hand, "You're coming with me. Everyone thinks I've lost my mind."

He shook his head, "They will have to continue to think that because I only wanted to come here to apologize for deceiving you. I should have told you that I was in Switzerland. Then you would have known I was alive and I'd be back to take my rightful place. I'm sorry."

"Why? Why weren't you in that car with me? Who was that?"

"Who he was doesn't really matter now. I had gone to get my back fixed, and with all the death threats, I never dreamed the top would be down on the car. I thought he'd be safe." John stared at her in earnestness.

"It would have been a nice thing to know." She stared back at him as some of the bitterness and hate dissolved, "You've made a fine mess of things. What do you plan to do now?"

"I'm not really sure. I may go to one of the safe houses the government has and live my life out there. I won't bother you again. You're still free to do what you want. Please, don't marry Onassis. He's evil."

"Like you said, you have no claim to me and you didn't really care about it when you did. I'll marry who I please and who will provide the best for the kids." Jackie bowed up, looking for a fight.

"Are the kids okay? I miss them every day." Jack lowered his head.

"They're fine. Growing and healing from their loss."

Jack wiped at a single tear, "Don't think this isn't unbearable for me. I've lost my family, my career, and who I was. I'm suffering too. Just remember that when you tuck them in at night. Tell them good things about their father because I do love them."

She let go of his hand at last, "I do that every chance I get. It expands the Camelot myth. Have a nice life, John." She turned and walked away.

Onassis finished his shower and went down to meet up with the acting king of Saudi Araba, Faisal Saud. Saud was waiting for him on the balcony of the morning room.

Ari walked up to him, "Good morning, King Saud."

Laughing, Prince Faisal replied, "No, no. I am only a regent as of yet. My brother has not yet stepped down officially."

A shocked Onassis stared at his guest. "I thought all of that had been settled?"

"Soon my friend, soon. It is a pleasant enough morning, a bit humid for my liking but I guess beauty deserves moisture." He was staring out at the water gently lapping onto the sand. The view was gorgeous with lots of vivid flowers and fully budding trees.

"True. I'd like to talk business if we could."

The prince turned to face him, "I'm going to presume about oil?"

Ari chuckled, "Yes. As you know the U.S. government already thwarted me once, and it cost me a hell of a lot more than the seven million in fines. But that is past and now I am in a position to once again end the U.S.'s monopoly on Saudi oil."

"How do you propose to do this?" Prince Saud raised an eyebrow.

"You may remember my associate from my whaling days, Hjalmar Schact?"

"Yes."

"He is helping finance this deal. I'll have our man's backing. And we both know the U.S. can't balk at that."

"You think that your German friend has that much sway?"

"I know he does. He's a huge financier on the world's stage and the U.S. will know this is a legitimate deal." Onassis got out his cigarette case and offered one to the prince. He declined, so Ari lit one up and waited.

"I'll go along with you as far as this will take us." Prince Saud turned back to his beautiful view, effectively dismissing Onassis.

"Have a wonderful weekend. If you need anything, you need only ask a member of my staff."

J. Edgar Hoover entered the lobby of the Hotel Del Charro in Coronado, California with his aide, Clyde. They were both dressed in the business suits they had traveled in. Hoover took a seat while Clyde dealt with checking in, luggage, and other little details. He watched as several other people came and went.

"Edgar, I'm so glad that you could make it." Cole Porter shook his hand. "I've got us the best rooms, all suites, and we're going to have a terrific time this evening. We've even got a piano in the suite. They are so accommodating here."

"Didn't I tell you friends would do whatever was necessary to make it a pleasant experience?" Hoover smiled.

"Yes, Clint Murchison told me he was from Texas. How did you come to know him?"

"The President has known him for years and recommended this place when he heard I was taking a short vacation. Apparently they were oil men in Texas before Clint bought the Del Charro" Hoover smiled and stood up as Clyde joined them.

"Cole, good to see you." The two men shook hands.

"Be sure to dress up this evening. It's not a casual affair. I've also got us some really nice guests to help us enjoy the party. See you at eight."

Cole Porter headed out the door as the two FBI men went to the elevator. Clyde punched the button and asked, "What do you think he's up to?"

They got into the empty elevator, "I don't know but it sounds delicious."

Chapter 19

Bobby and Stansel walked into the conference room at the police station. Kennedy was greeted by everyone as he entered but he went straight to Norma. "It's so good to see you again." Bobby gave her a tight hug and then turned to Bill, "Walton, thank you for taking such good care of our girl."

Bill smiled and put his arm around Norma, "It was my pleasure. She is a trooper."

Bobby agreed, "Don't I know it." Kennedy looked around. He spotted Latimer, "Where's Jack?"

Latimer heard the question and hurried over to the trio. "He had an errand to run. He said he'd be back soon."

Alarm bells went off in Bobby's head, "What kind of errand?"

"He didn't really say. He did say he wanted some decent coffee." Latimer shrugged.

"How did he leave here? Did he walk?" Bobby asked.

"No, sir, I gave him the keys and he drove." Latimer started to look uncomfortable. "Should I have gone with him?"

"Very possibly. I guess we'll find out when he returns." Kennedy turned back to the group and walked to the front of the room where there was a chalk board and notebooks piled up in a stack.

"Everyone, let me have your attention."

Once the room had gotten quiet and all were settled, Bobby began, "Now as you know we have a Haitian prince on our soil. This same man engineered the kidnapping of Norma Baker and took her out of the country. The fact that Bill Walton managed to go with her was a miracle or we probably would never have seen her again."

Everybody applauded. Bobby waited, "Now, we need to decide what information we want from him and how best to get it out of him. Just to be clear here, I'm all for torture in this case."

Mary sat at Pat's kitchen table eating a late breakfast of Cheerios and milk. Pat was reading a book and drinking a cup of coffee, "Did you sleep okay in a strange bed?"

"I could have slept on a rock and been perfectly comfortable I was so exhausted from missing sleep the night before. It's so great of you to let me stay here."

"It's my pleasure I've been a little bored and depressed. It's good to have company." Pat got up and refilled her mug.

The phone rang, "Hello?" Pat picked up the receiver hanging on the wall beside her.

"Pat? It's Ethel. How are things going?"

"Oh, hey Ethel, things are great. We're just in the kitchen doing breakfast. You know, we slept really late this morning."

"I'm glad. I thought you might sleep in, so I waited to call. Bobby is busy with work and of course I'm just sitting here at the hotel, bored. I have a good mind to go raid the gift shop and charge a bunch of stuff. Maybe I should go to the beautician and have my hair done. Her shop looked nice as we passed by last night."

"I think you should. You deserve a little pampering with all that's been on your shoulders lately." Pat agreed.

"How's Mary this morning?"

"She's good, do you want to talk to her?" Pat walked over to Mary and handed her the phone.

"Um, no that's not necessary." Ethel said.

"Hello? It's Mary. Sorry, but Pat just gave you to me."

"No problem. Are you okay?"

"Yes. I feel safe here. It's wonderful. I doubt there are prying eyes looking for me here"

"I'm sure you're safe. I'll call you when I get back. It'll be Monday morning before I'll have the opportunity, more than likely."

"Thanks Ethel, for everything."

"Tell Pat good bye for me."

"Ethel says 'bye'." Mary informed Pat as both women hung up.

"Great. So, what are you wanting to do today?" Pat sat down with the paper and her coffee mug.

"I'm at your mercy. Is there a good movie playing right now? I could use a distraction." Mary drank the milk in her cereal bowl then took it to the sink.

"Mary Poppins just came out yesterday. You may not want to see that though."

"Naw, what else is out?"

"Let's see, how about 'Send Me No Flowers' or 'Sex and the Single Girl'?"

"Either sounds good and maybe some pizza." Mary smiled and got up. "I'll go shower and get ready. My treat."

President Johnson found his wife in the library playing cards with Cary Grant, Ava Gabor, and Frank

Sinatra. He walked over and kissed her on the top of the head. "I'll be in the garden if you want to join me later."

Lady Bird glanced away from her hand and looked at her husband, "I'm sure this will last for a while. You go ahead and do whatever you'd like today. I'll see you at dinner, for sure."

Johnson walked away puzzled. He was scratching his head when he walked into a wall. One of the staff snickered and hurried away.

Prince Rainier had just come in through the French doors that led out to the garden area.

"Prince Rainier, how are you?" Lyndon asked louder than necessary.

The prince looked amused, "I am good. How are you?"

Johnson looked sheepish, "Fine. I guess my judgment is a little off today."

"Well then, no national crisis' or major decisions should be your rule. We all need time away to just be human. The burden we carry sometimes weighs entirely too much." Rainier sympathized.

"Too true. Would you join me for a drink? I thought I saw the makings for a screw driver on the waiters' trays."

"Of course, but you must promise me there will be no talk of politics, just pleasant conversation about ordinary topics. How do you like the new television shows? I was watching 'The Twilight Zone' with your Rod Sterling the other evening and I was completely mesmerized by it."

Johnson and Rainier strolled outside in the fresh air and took a drink from the tray. After a while they decided to sit beside the pool and watch the stunning Greek women frolic in the water.

"You're right, Prince Rainier, this is a most excellent way to pass the day." Johnson beckoned to a twenty something lady who had just entered the pool area in a white string bikini, which showed off her dark coloring and figure.

Prince Rainier excused himself and left the President of the United States flirting shamelessly with someone who wasn't his wife. He smiled as he walked away, *Boys will be boys no matter where or what nation they come from.*

While Kennedy finished talking to the men who were to torture Papa Doc, Stansel motioned for Walton to join him. He opened the door and led Bill into the hall. "I just wanted to let you know that we've taken a lot of heat for the slow reaction time we had when JFK was assassinated. We can no longer drive with a top down, we must be alert at all times, and protect the President whether we like him or not. We're also no longer allowed to operate as a rogue agency. We must give an accurate accounting to the President or Attorney General when we're asked."

Bill sighed, "So we have to watch our step in the American political arena. What about foreign?"

"We still have free reign there. The less our leaders know the better as long as we're protecting our country." Stansel moved aside as the door opened to Bobby leaving the room.

"I have to get back to the wife. She's always complaining we don't spend enough time together, but God knows we must because we have eight children and we're expecting again."

Jack sat in the car on the side of the highway stunned by his encounter with Jackie. He had his head on the steering wheel while the car idled. After several moments, he pulled himself together, shrugged it off, and pulled back onto the highway. He turned on the radio. The Supremes were singing the number one hit of the summer, "Where Did Our Love Go".

"How appropriate. Where did our love go?" He hollered out the window as he banged his hand on the steering wheel. *We never had a love. Our lives were a lie. A match made because my dad needed a beautiful, well-bred girl to make my image complete.*

He turned into the parking lot of the police precinct as Bobby came out the front doors. He parked the car and got out. Bobby noticed the look on Jack's face.

"I can only guess that whatever hair brained idea you had, seeing Jackie didn't go as planned?"

"No. I thought it would be bad but I had to see her. She was, as usual, her kind and gracious self." Sarcasm simply dripped from Jack's words.

"I'm sorry, Jack." Bobby actually patted him on the arm. "I want you to torment Duvalier for me, but I think Ethel would kill me if I didn't bring you back to see her. Mary told her you were alive and boy was she furious with me."

"I can imagine." Jack laughed as he got into Bobby's car. The keys jabbed into his thigh in his pocket, "Oh wait, I have Latimer's keys."

"He's not going anywhere at present, he's got his assignment." Bobby put the car in reverse and they headed back to the hotel.

"So what do you want me to do to Duvalier?"

Walter Jenkins found Lyndon sitting at the pool talking to a stunning Greek goddess in a string bikini. She was practically sitting on his lap on the lounger. He was relaxed and laughed at something she said in heavily accented English.

Walter walked over to the bar at the edge of the pool area. The view was magnificent as the waves rolled lazily onto the shore beyond the garden. He ordered a screwdriver and glanced around as he waited for the bartender to fix it. Most of the guests were sunning with eyes closed, drowsy from the partying last night and the warm sun.

The Greek goddess got up and left the President as Jenkins took his drink from the bar keep and headed over to his old friend.

"You look happy." Jenkins settled himself in the lounger next to Johnson.

"A beautiful woman's attention will do that for an old man."

"I understand Onassis and McIntyre had a meeting this morning. Do you know if they came to an agreement?" Jenkins sipped his screwdriver and pushed his sunglasses back up onto the bridge of his nose.

"No, I haven't seen either one of them since I came down. It would help us out if McIntyre would cooperate with a dock for Onassis, but I don't see the American public standing for it. Everyone hates him."

"We need a way to change his image. I know he's a shrewd, if not ruthless business man, but he always does what he says he will do. That kind of integrity should be worth something." Jenkins nodded at a beautiful blonde who was passing by them.

"It's not really integrity. It's more like bulldogging. Once he sinks his teeth into an idea he won't give up until he gets what he wants."

"Sometimes you don't get what you want. What does he do then?"

"He sends someone in who will be able to get it done." Johnson shook his head, "Being in business with Onassis can be terrifying."

Chapter 20

Mary waited while Pat closed the front door. The girls were laughing and ready for a fun day with no stress. As they turned to go down the sidewalk to the car, a black sedan pulled up in the driveway.

"Oh no!" Pat threw a hand up to her mouth.

"I don't want to go back." Mary clutched Pat's arm.

Two secret service men got out of the car and walked up to them. "Mary Meyer?" the taller of the two asked.

Mary nodded, "That's me."

"Good day to you, we've been assigned to keep you safe. We're to escort you wherever you wish to go." He stuck out his hand, "I'm Joshua Smith and this is my partner, Randy Wesson."

Mary laughed out loud, "Smith and Wesson?"

Bobby pulled the car up to the valet at the hotel. Jack got out and stretched.

"Jack!" Ethel came running out of the double glass doors leading into the hotel, "OH Jack!"

He turned in time for her to throw herself into his arms, sobbing with joy. "I've missed you so much."

161

Jack folded her into an embrace, "Hi Ethel." He looked a bit sheepish, "It's good to see you too."

She stepped back, "Let me look at you." She scanned him up and down, "I can't believe it's really you."

"It's really me. I'm sorry for the distress I caused you. I hope you will forgive the ruse." Jack kissed her cheek.

"You, I forgive, but it'll be awhile before Bobby gets the same relief." Ethel took his arm, "Let's go get some coffee and catch up."

Bobby followed behind them, shaking his head. Ethel was chattering away about the family as Jack leaned his head in towards her. They walked at a sedate pace, while she clung to her brother-in-law as if life depended on it.

Onassis had just left Maria Callas' room and was heading back down the hallway when he spotted Jackie going into her room. "Are you still angry with me?" He caught up to her and followed her inside the room.

"Yes, even more now that I've seen you leaving Maria." Jackie folded her arms.

"You know I'm never faithful to one woman. I won't be faithful to you when we're married, though it will be more discreet." Ari moved to the small settee near a window.

"I won't be faithful to you either, so what?" Jackie didn't budge.

"Now that we've settled that, why are you still angry?" Ari sat down and crossed his leg.

"You know very well. It's Christina."

"Yes, the ever present problem child. I don't believe she is really why you're angry." Ari inspected his finger nails.

"True. It's *you* I'm upset with. We can't have a relationship if the girl is going to be disrespectful and rude to me. I should at least have you defend me."

Jackie moved over to the high backed straight chair and sat on the edge.

"What did she say that wasn't true?" Ari waited a moment, "Would you have me discipline her for speaking the truth?"

"Yes." Jackie stomped a foot to make the point clear.

"Well, I took care of it." Ari stomped his foot and walked away.

Bobby sat listening to Ethel and Jack for a solid hour before he interrupted. "I think it's time to get Jack back to the police station. He has something to do there."

Ethel pouted, "I'm not ready to give him up yet."

Jack smiled and patted her arm, "I'll see you this evening. Let's all go have dinner."

"Can we?" Ethel sounded like a child.

Bobby nodded his head, "Yes, of course we can. I'll get us a private room at the swanky place down the road. What are your plans for the afternoon?"

"I think I'll take a nap," Ethel rubbed her growing tummy, "The baby seems to be tired."

Bobby stood up and kissed her head, "Yes, I'm sure that he is."

As they left the coffee shop, Jack leaned down and kissed the top of Ethel's head, "You're a trooper. Why anyone would want to breed with this goon is a mystery to me. You married the wrong brother, you know that don't you?"

Ethel smiled at him as she blushed, "Always a flirt, aren't you?" She turned toward the lobby, "I'll see you this evening."

Bobby followed her, caught her in his arms, and hugged her tightly. "I love you." He kissed her soundly.

"Well, your dead brother should come back from the dead more often." She grinned, "Maybe I don't need a nap after all."

"I'll hurry back." Bobby patted her butt, "I'll wake you with a little surprise." He grinned, winked at her and strode back to Jack.

Papa Doc watched warily as Jack made his way toward him. A chair had been placed outside his cell and Jack sat down on it. He sat and waited. Papa Doc remained silent. Five minutes, then ten went by without a word between them.

After fifteen minutes had passed, Duvalier stood up and stormed around his cell. "Talk if you must, but don't just sit there watching me like I'm an animal at the zoo."

"Actually, the zoo is more entertaining." Jack stood up and faced Papa Doc.

"What do you want?" Papa Doc came closer and put his hands around the bars. "Are you going to tell me that you're not John F. Kennedy?"

Jack watched him for a good two minutes before he answered, "No."

"I knew it. You are the President. Now I've got you!" Papa Doc did a little jig around his tiny cell.

"Actually, it is I who have you." Jack walked away.

Bill and Norma sat on the beach watching the people splash in the surf. Norma squished her bare toes into the sand and sighed. Bill opened the picnic basket and dug out some fried chicken.

"It was great that the hotel has picnic lunches for 'romantic dates on the beach'." Bill laughed as he bit into the juicy chicken leg. He wiped his mouth with a cloth napkin. Children were laughing and running past them.

Norma ignored the kids and glanced over to him, she gave him a quick smile. She turned her attention back to her feet. Bill watched her for a minute, put his chicken bone back in the plastic container, and took a swig of beer.

"Honey, what's wrong?" He touched her thigh gently to get her full attention.

"Sitting here reminds me of when Peter told me that I was 'dead'. It's a strange feeling to know that you'll never be who you were." Norma dug her toes further into the sand and looked over at Bill. "I would love to have Maf, and my books. Oh, how I miss those. I know I'll never get my home or things back but there are treasures I miss." She blinked back tears.

"Oh, Norma," Bill moved closer to her and placed his arm around her shoulder. "I can't imagine how hard this has been for you. I've never heard you complain about any of it. You know you can talk to me."

She turned her face into his shoulder and allowed herself to sob. After several minutes, she lifted her face and he handed her a napkin. She blew her nose into it and placed it under her thigh on the sand.

"I know things have to change, even when you just get to live your life but why does it have to be so difficult? Sometimes I wonder what would have happened if I hadn't been home that night. Would they have come after me anyway?" Norma sniffed.

"Probably." Bill squeezed her shoulder.

"It was my own damn fault. I was so mad at Jack for dumping me without a word that I had called a press conference to rat out his evil ways. It would have been a huge scandal and ruined any chance Edward had for getting a Senate seat. I was spiteful and vindictive. Hate causes people to do stupid things." Norma shook her head at her own idiocy.

"He should have let you know that he was done, it was cowardly. Didn't Bobby come tell you in the end?"

Norma played with the sand, allowing it to sift through her fingers, "Yes, he did, but he wasn't nice about it. Basically, leave my brother alone or else. I had to let them know they couldn't intimidate me, but I was wrong, they could and they did. Joe Kennedy is bigger than me."

"It's true. They are motivated by the patriarch of the family." Bill rubbed her shoulders.

"Yes, Daddy ran with the likes of Al Capone and made his wealth the old fashioned mob style way. He ran boot legging with Capone, among other things. He wants the boys in politics so guess where they are? Family loyalty is a foreign concept for me." Norma sighed, "But we all have to move on."

"Let's move on together, honey. Let's get married and move anywhere you want, but far, far away from anything Hollywood, political or depressing. You've the right to live a happy life. So what do you say?" Bill turned her face to his with a gentle hand, "Will you marry me? You are my heart and soul. I can't live without you and I'll make you happy, or try to, until my dying day."

Jack returned to the conference room chuckling, Bobby had left him at the station and went back to spend time with Ethel. Stansel and Latimer were sitting at the big oval table with feet propped up, eating pizza. Jack grabbed a slice out of the box at one end of the table and slapped it on a paper plate. He grabbed a cup of coffee and sat down.

"Coffee and pizza? Where's the beer?" Jack asked as he settled into a leather chair.

"We were lucky to get pizza." Stansel looked up from the paper he'd been reading. "Apparently, there was a standing O for Mr. Kennedy at the convention."

"Can I see that? I haven't read a newspaper in ages." Jack leaned forward to take the paper from Stansel. He skimmed the headlines and then read the article in detail. His eyes filled with tears as he adjusted the paper to cover his face. "Wow, JFK was well loved it seems."

"Of course," Latimer chimed in, "it didn't hurt that he was killed during his presidency and now is a legend."

Jack re-read the article. "I wonder what Bobby was thinking that whole time. It seems like standing there for over twenty minutes would be difficult."

"Not when it's full blown adoration. Look at this from the Times. 'Kennedy nearly cried'."

Stansel passed him the other section of paper. Jack took it and skimmed the article.

"How did it go with Duvalier?" Latimer broke Jack's concentration.

"I did just what I was told. It seemed to freak him out." Jack put the papers aside and ate his pizza.

"You're on again in ten minutes. Here are the questions you need to ask him." Latimer slid a yellow legal pad down the table. Jack caught it and picked it up.

"Got it." He nodded when he finished the list. "This should be interesting."

Chapter 21

Barbara and Gregory made their way down the beach toward Norma and Bill. "Norma will be so surprised to see me!" Barbara nearly squealed with excitement.

Gregory smiled and took her hand. The sunlight caught the huge diamond glistening on the ring finger of her left hand as he brought it firmly into his. "That's not all that will surprise her."

Onassis sat across from Prince Rainer. "I think you understand why I would like to build hotels and casinos in Monaco? We could make it like Vegas only without the restrictions. People love evil and they love sin. Let's give it to them in spades."

Prince Rainer stroked his cheek for a moment, "What do I get out of the deal?"

Onassis laughed, "For one thing, I won't kill you for squelching the deal in Italy and for another, you will receive a cut of the profits. Tourism will go up and the rich will want to come to Monaco for vacations. I'll bring Jacquelyn for the grand opening and that will in turn rake in the elite in America. You can't lose with this deal."

The prince sat for a moment, "Hmm, with you there is always an element of risk. However, yes. Let's move forward on this."

"I'm going to resign when we get back to D.C." Bobby stroked Ethel's naked back as he pulled the covers up over her bare body.

"It's about time." She turned her face up to his. He kissed her.

"I've been thinking that we could use Jack to help me with Johnson."

Ethel leaned up on an elbow, "How would you do that?"

"Since Jack is alive he is still technically the President. Johnson is usurping his position." Bobby sat up. "Jack could go to him and tell him he can still look like the President, but things need to be done his way or he'll 'return from the dead'."

"Do you think Johnson will be so easily cowed? The man is as stubborn as an ox and meaner than anyone I know." Ethel sat up and gathered her scattered undergarments.

"Johnson is a mean, bitter, vicious – an animal in many ways. He lies all the time, even when he doesn't have to. He's all about the power and money, he doesn't want to have to step back now. That's why I think this will work." Bobby sounded more certain than he felt.

"I hope you're right. What did Jack say about this scheme?" Ethel picked up her dress and headed into the bathroom to start the shower.

"I haven't told him yet."

Mary and Pat had enjoyed a movie and dinner at a nice restaurant. Smith and Wesson had driven them around town and now were standing guard outside of Pat's house. Mary finished her wine as they watched television.

"I know I have to leave you, but I don't want to go. This has been the most relaxing fun I've had in ages." Mary sighed and picked up her empty glass. She twirled it around her fingers for a second and then put it back on the coffee table.

Pat watched her. "I've enjoyed having you here. I needed a break as well and I couldn't have asked for a better companion. Why haven't we been friends all this time?"

"Jackie." They said in unison.

"I don't give a hang what she thinks anymore. I'd love to be friends." Mary sat up.

"Me too. I'll call you next week and we'll go to lunch." Pat smiled as Mary got up.

"I guess I'll get the bulldogs to take me home now. Smith and Wesson, what genius put the two of them together?" Mary laughed.

Pat got up and hugged her new friend. "I'll see you next week, okay?"

"Absolutely." Mary patted Pat's arm, then hesitated. "You don't know, do you?"

"Know what?"

"He's still alive."

"Who?" Pat looked puzzled.

"Your brother, Jack, he's still alive. He was in the Alps having back surgery but he didn't heal fast enough to return before the Amarillo trip. That man was his body double. It seems that Jackie knew all along that Jack was going to be assassinated but she didn't know the man was an imposter."

"Wait, go back. Jack's alive?"

"Yes. Ask Bobby where he is. I'd love to know. I think we can have a life together. I only told you because you have a right to know that I'm in love with Jack and I'll be around more often if things work out." Mary turned to open the front door.

Pat sat down as her legs suddenly gave way beneath her.

Papa Doc was asleep when Jack came back to the cell. He banged on the bars with an empty tin cup. Papa Doc nearly fell off the bed at the sudden noise.

Jack moved back a few steps as Duvalier lunged at him. "Is that anyway to act? What are you going to do, cast a voodoo spell on me? You are such a fraud."

Duvalier sneered at him, "Don't be too sure, I just might."

"Smoke and mirrors, no real power in your 'potions'. The only power is the poison you put in them. Should I mix one up for you?" Jack sat down in the hard metal folding chair outside of the cell.

"How did you know?"

"No one is as powerful as you claim to be. There is some merit in voodoo but you've twisted it into a power play for your own benefit."

"Your sources are ill informed, Kennedy."

"We'll see." Jack waited for a few minutes. Papa Doc grew restless.

"Why are you here?" Duvalier finally broke the silence.

"For information, of course. Let's start with an easy question. Why were you trying to find Marilyn Monroe? You know she's dead."

"Oh no she isn't and I know that for a fact."

"Really? How do you know anything for a fact? If you're referring to the woman you brought here to the Hamptons, she's not Monroe; she's just a terrified woman agreeing to whatever you say to keep from dying at your hand."

Norma had been coming out of the surf when she noticed a couple had joined Bill. *That's Barbara!* She ran up the beach to her friend. Barbara stood up and she hugged a dripping Norma.

"I can't believe it's you!" Barbara hugged Norma again.

"Oh, I've missed you. I've got so much to tell you." Norma began but noticed the huge ring on Barbara's finger. "It looks like you've got something to tell me as well."

Gregory stood up, "Norma this is Gregory Morris. Greg, Norma Baker. Greg was assigned to your case when you were kidnapped. We met when I gave him a statement." Barbara blushed. Bill also stood to greet the newcomers properly.

Gregory held out his hand, "It's nice to meet you. I've heard so much about you."

Norma laughed and hugged him, "I've heard nothing about you, but if Barbara loves you then I'm sure I will too."

The group sat back down on the quilt, all talking at once. They laughed and passed around beer. Bill held his bottle up as they all followed suit, "A toast, to old friends, new ones, and new beginnings." They clinked the bottles together and drank.

Bill smiled, "We have news as well. Maybe we could have a double wedding?"

"Norma! Congratulations!" Barbara flung herself across the quilt and hugged her friend in a tight embrace. "Have you made any plans?"

"No, I just accepted this afternoon. Have you made plans?" Norma leaned closer to Bill when Barbara moved back over to Greg.

"I'm planning on retiring." Greg volunteered, "I'm hoping to get some land somewhere and maybe ranch. Cattle or sheep."

"That sounds wonderful!" Norma leaned closer to Bill, "We're still in the talking stage. I have no idea what we'll do."

Barbara took a swig of her beer, "Whatever you decide, we need to be close. I can't imagine not being near my best friend."

Norma glanced at Bill, and he smiled, "I'm game if you are. What do you think, Greg?"

"As long as this lady is happy, so am I."

Norma spoke up, "I want to live in Texas. It is the perfect place to have a ranch. There's wide open spaces and lots of great things to do in the metropolitan areas."

Her excitement was infectious. They sat and planned until the sun went down. Bill stood up and gathered up the picnic supplies while Gregory and Barbara shook out the quilt. "Let's get cleaned up and go have dinner. My treat." Bill suggested.

The women linked arms and happily headed up the beach to the parking lot. Bill watched Norma as he said to Greg, "I guess we'd better become friends, it looks like those two are going to be just like Lucy and Ethel."

Greg laughed out loud, and the girls turned back to look but kept walking. Greg waved them on.

Mary stood outside of her house with Smith while Wesson checked inside to make sure all was clear. Wesson opened the door and motioned them in.

As she stepped inside, she stopped in her tracks and looked around at all the chaos.

Wesson stepped over to her, "I'm sorry, but the whole place has been tossed. We'll put the furniture back if you'll tell us where it goes."

Mary slid down the doorframe and took a deep breath. The agents began picking up the end tables, then the couch. Smith replaced the cushions on the sofa while Wesson set the rocking chair back in the corner.

She got up and began the long process of cleaning up scattered papers, belongings and trash.

"Our agents wouldn't have done this." Smith told her.

Wesson nodded, "This was a hit from the mob, most likely."

"What does that mean?" Mary turned to them.

"It means they really want whatever it is they were looking for. It's possible that there's a mole in the agency." Smith flipped over a footstool.

Chapter 22

<u>September 1, 1964</u>

Papa Doc was awakened at two in the morning with a bright light shining in his eyes and a loud noise blaring through speakers like static. He sat up and covered his eyes with a forearm. He yelled out, "What the Hell are you doing?" but no one answered.

The noise and lights went off without warning. Duvalier waited but all was silent. He settled back down and went to sleep. At three a.m. the same thing happened. This went on every hour, on the hour, for the rest of the night. At seven, an agent came near the cell and handed him a cup of diluted coffee and a donut.

Duvalier sat down with his measly breakfast. The agent watched him munch his donut but said nothing. After the tiny paper cup was empty, Papa Doc walked over to the agent and handed the cup through the bars of his cell.

"Could I have a refill?" he asked.

The agent crumpled the cup, threw it in the metal trash can, and walked away.

"Damn it, a person can't live on this little bit of nothing! I demand more coffee." Papa Doc turned back to his bed and sat down exhausted. He slumped back against the wall and waited.

The agent returned with a fresh cup and handed it silently through the bars to Duvalier.

Duvalier took a peek inside the cup. "What the hell, these are the grounds. I asked for coffee."

The agent shrugged and took his seat.

"I see how this game is going to be played. Prolonged suffering followed by torture and then I'll talk. Why doesn't anyone ask me a question? I never said I wouldn't talk."

The agent picked up a newspaper and began reading it.

"You fucking idiot, talk to me. Tell me something. I will not be ignored."

The agent turned the page and continued to read, unfazed by the outburst.

Ari watched Cary Grant as he walked along the beach with the Gabor sisters. He hadn't been able to talk to Grant since his arrival. It seemed that he had avoided Onassis his whole visit.

Frank Sinatra joined the trio on the beach. They were laughing at something Frank had said. Onassis watched them for a moment with a wrinkled brow. *I'll win you over. You'll be eating out of my hand when I'm through.*

Jack was sitting in the conference room waiting for Latimer to come back from messing with Papa Doc. Bobby poked his head in the door, saw Jack and came in. Stansel was sitting at the other end of the table doing a cross word puzzle.

Bobby sat next to his brother, "I think I'm going to resign my position tomorrow. If we can come up with a game plan, we can make Johnson squirm. There is really nothing I'd rather see than him taken down a few pegs. Are you in?"

Jack grinned, "Of course I'm in. Once this Papa Doc mess is finished. I'll come to D.C. and we'll meet up to talk. I think we should have Norma, Bill, and of course, your two sidekicks as well."

"I agree. I'll see you later in the week. I'm heading back to Ethel and we're taking a jet back to the capital." Bobby stood up, shook Jack's hand and spoke briefly to Stansel before he left.

Jacquelyn Kennedy was sitting in the dining room when Maria Callas strolled in. Lunch was in the process of being dished up. Maria sat down across the table from Jackie. Most of the party was out on the beach which left only a few people at the table.

Maria smiled at Jackie, "How are you?"

Jackie looked up, her expression showing her offense at being spoken to at all. "Fine."

"Aren't you just a happy girl today? What's the matter darling, aren't you getting enough attention from our host?" Maria accepted a small salad and dinner roll from the waiter.

"I'm getting as much as I like." Jackie's face flamed.

"Women who are satisfied aren't usually so catty."

Jackie stood up and stormed out of the room while Maria softly chuckled at her small victory.

Norma met Bill at the little café in the hotel lobby. Bill kissed her, took her hand, and led her into the restaurant. "I've missed you." He nuzzled her ear and she giggled.

"Not as much as I missed you." Norma told him automatically, *but I really mean it. I've been with so many men, I've developed rehearsed lines.* She squeezed his hand a little tighter.

The hostess seated them at a little booth with a view of the garden.

"I'm so hungry." Bill picked up the menu as the waitress came over.

"Coffee for us both, please."

The waitress placed two glasses of ice water in front of them. "Are you ready to order?"

"Not yet." Norma smiled at her.

"Take your time. I'll go get the coffee."

Once they made their choices and the waitress had gone to tell the kitchen, they linked hands across the table.

"I'd like to make plans to get married. It'll be small, but it can be elegant or whatever you want. However, it needs to be soon." Bill gazed lovingly at her.

"Aren't you the eager one?" She smiled and averted her gaze for a second. Then batted her eyelashes at him. He laughed.

"Yes, I'm eager. I've been waiting for you to realize I loved you for a while now. For me, it's been an eternity and I'm ready to have and to hold you forever." Bill let go of her hand and moved over beside her. He put his arm around her shoulder. "How about today?"

Norma kissed his cheek. "I'll need to think about it. I've been married before you know."

The waitress placed their steaming plates in front of them, "Is there anything else?"

"No, thank you." Bill smiled as she topped off the coffee cups.

"Holler if you need something."

Bill turned to Norma. "It's true that *Marilyn Monroe* has been married before, but Norma Baker hasn't. This is different, this is forever, and this is with *me*."

Norma thought about what he just said as she sipped her coffee. She suddenly looked up and nearly screamed, "Then let's go to Vegas!"

"Really?" Bill laughed.

"Yes! I don't want to wait either. I'll call Barbara and see if they can go with us. We'll need witnesses." Norma giggled and dove into her pancakes with gusto.

Jack Lancer approached the cell where Duvalier was sleeping. He took the tin cup off of the chair and ran it over the bars. Papa Doc jumped at the sudden racket and turned to glare at the offender.

"Kennedy! I wanted to see you." He came over to the bars and stood glaring at Jack.

"You wanted to see me?"

"Yes. Let me out of here!"

"Such demands from a prisoner. It's crazy. I've had a nice vat of sulfuric acid prepared for you. That is your favorite way to torture your enemies, isn't it?"

Papa Doc blanched. He thought for a second, "Now look, we don't need to get nasty over this shit, do we?"

"Or do we?"

"No, not at all. What do you want to know?"

"What can you tell me about Onassis? I don't want public knowledge, I want back deals."

Papa Doc grinned, "I can tell you a few things if you want dirt on him."

"That's what I want." Jack picked at a loose thread on his shirt cuff.

"I'm sure you know that Onassis and Johnson are in cahoots. Why do you think LBJ was able to reverse your Vietnam policy so quickly?"

"How?"

"The new bill was ready to go two days after your death. Doesn't that seem a bit strange? Congress doesn't work that quickly unless there is a ton of money and other incentives offered. "

"Do you know who was behind the assassination?" Jack watched Duvalier closely.

"Of course, but that information isn't for sale."

"Have it your way. I'll have the agents come and take you to that vat."

Lady Bird stood outside the mansion with her husband, "Must we leave so soon? I was having a wonderful time."

"Yes, I have business in Washington and we need to get back."

"Why can't you go alone or send Jenkins?"

Johnson lost patience, "Woman, I'm the President and you're the First Lady. Now stop arguing and get in the limo. You have duties to attend to as well as I do."

The driver opened the door as Lyndon shoved his wife into the seat.

Onassis had stood to the side during this exchange, "Johnson."

"Onassis, thank you for inviting us. You are, as ever, a superb host." Johnson held out his hand to Onassis. They shook.

"Thank you. I know we'll meet again soon. This weekend has been a success in all ways."

Johnson understood his meaning, "Good to hear."

Chapter 23

<u>September 3, 1964</u>

Robert Kennedy walked into the Oval Office late in the day. He handed Lyndon Johnson his resignation. The President read it, "I accept."

Bobby turned on his heel and walked out of the office without a word to his sworn enemy.

J. Edgar Hoover waited for Bobby outside on the White House steps. Bobby was surprised to see him. "What are you doing here?"

"Looking for you." Hoover shook Kennedy's hand as they walked down the steps.

"How did you know where I was?" Bobby asked then laughed, "Stupid question, you're the head of the FBI, you 'have your ways'."

"Indeed I do. It seems we have an unfinished conversation we need to pick up. The last time we spoke, you dropped a bombshell on me and then ran home to some family crisis."

Bobby turned down the sidewalk with Hoover at his side, "Sorry about that. These death threats are wigging out my wife and she's in a delicate condition so I feel obligated to take care of her fears."

"Understandable. Now can we discuss the JFK topic?" Hoover lit a cigarette and offered Bobby one out of the pack.

"Sure. I've just resigned my position so I don't care if the world implodes, it's not my problem." Bobby lit his cigarette, inhaled deeply and blew out a cleansing breath.

Hoover waited for a moment. "Where has he been?"

"Hiding in plain sight. He had his appearance altered slightly, grew a mustache and a goatee, put on some glasses, and boom he's Jack Lancer."

Hoover shook his head, "Master of disguises? Clever. What's he been doing?"

"He's been helping me out here and there. We had a hard time finding a way to keep him busy but I finally got it. He's the one who went and rescued Georgi." Bobby stopped walking when they reached the park and sat down on a bench. Hoover took the empty spot next to Kennedy.

"Where was he since he wasn't in the motorcade?" Hoover swatted at a piece of blowing paper.

"Switzerland. He had back surgery after his tour in Germany. We had a double get off the plane and no one was the wiser."

"But he is rightfully still the President of the United States. Why hasn't he come forward and explained it was all a mistake?" Hoover shook his head, "I can't make sense of it."

"A couple of reasons: one, it would look bad to the public; two, it wouldn't have been a good political move to have his world counter parts see him as weak. He didn't want anyone to know he had a bad back and that's why it was secret in the first place. You know how finicky the world is. They don't like cowards or weaklings." Kennedy stopped for a moment, "But most importantly, he didn't want to ruin his legacy and the Camelot fantasy created on his behalf. Let the people mourn him as a hero but at a great personal sacrifice to him. He lost his whole world."

Hoover nodded, "That makes sense in a twisted sort of way. I'll have to accept it. So what now?"

"We're planning on taking him to a safe house to live out his days in privacy."

Hoover stood up, "I have to go, but next time we talk about Monroe."

"There's nothing to talk about there. She's changed her appearance and moved to a foreign country. She just wants to be left alone."

"Fair enough." Hoover walked away.

Bill and Norma waited in front of the Little White Wedding Chapel for Barbara and Gregory to catch up with them. They'd all left the Marriage License Bureau at the same time. As they walked along Las Vegas Boulevard, they came across a lovely jewelry store where the couples bought rings. Barbara was having a difficult time deciding on which necklace and earrings to choose to compliment the ring Greg had given her.

"I wish she would hurry," Bill watched the shop with great interest.

"She's a woman, so it may take her a while." Norma giggled. "Let's go in and get a head start on what they offer here."

Bill led her up the steps into the chapel. His grin was so wide that all of his teeth were showing. He couldn't seem to stop smiling. They walked up to the receptionist and asked for a brochure.

They discussed the options, both of them, and decided just as Barbara and Greg came in.

"Sorry. We had to get just the right ring for Greg." Barbara was glowing.

Norma hugged her. "Of course you did! We've decided what ceremony we'd like. What do you think of a double wedding?"

"Perfect!" Greg and Barbara shouted together.

"Great. Let's go get married." Bill led Norma over to the receptionist and pointed to their choice on the brochure. "We'd like a double wedding, please."

She grinned. "Right this way."

Barbara squeezed Greg's arm so tight he yelped, "Careful woman, you don't want to break it before you get a chance to see what it can do. That's for the honeymoon." He kissed her forehead.

Barbara blushed as they stood before the minister and vowed to love one another forever.

"Wait!" Papa Doc screamed, "It was Johnson. He wanted the conflict in Vietnam turned into war! You were pulling men out. He couldn't let that happen. Are you listening? He and Onassis want to run guns and munitions to the region and gain a fortune. Onassis is also into the drug trade, but I don't think Johnson is involved in that."

Jack turned to listen to Duvalier. He had walked back over to the cell as Papa Doc finished spilling his guts. "I've truly never met a more cowardly man than you, Duvalier. You enjoy torturing, acting like God and terrorizing everyone who doesn't do your bidding, but one hint at the idea of those same methods being used on you, and you cave! You're pathetic."

Jack turned on his heel and walked away.

Johnson called Nicholas Katzenbach into his office, "You will be acting Attorney General until someone is appointed to the position after the election and I, I mean the new President, takes office in January."

Katzenbach stood for a moment in shock, "Yes, Mr. President."

"Good. You start tomorrow when I will officially announce it." Johnson waited for him to leave. Nicholas just stood there, "You may go."

"Yes, Mr. President."

Mary Meyer returned to work. She typed up a letter and placed it in an envelope which she then mailed to Ethel Kennedy.

Dear Ethel,

If you read the dairy, you will find that Johnny Roselli was the shooter on the grassy knoll. I overheard Cord and Onassis discussing it after the assassination. Please get this information to the proper people in the event of my death.

Oswald was a dupe to divert attention from Roselli and Meyer Lansky, who actually shot Connolly through the windshield from the grassy knoll. They were all working for the CIA, Onassis, and Johnson. Ask Madeleine Brown about her knowledge of Johnson's involvement.

Yours, Mary Meyer

Norma and Bill Walton left the Wedding Chapel with Barbara and Greg Morris. They stepped into a waiting cab and went to the Dessert Inn for their respective honeymoons.

Bill held onto Norma's hand as they pulled up to the hotel. The cabbie got the bags out of the trunk of the car and handed them to a waiting bellhop. The newlyweds went inside to register.

"Mr. Walton, your room is ready and waiting." The clerk winked at Bill. Bill smiled and signed the register.

"Let's meet for dinner. What time?" Greg asked.

"We'll need at least a few hours." Bill answered unapologetically.

"So," Greg looked at his watch, "let's say eight?"

"That should do it. If we're not here go without us." Bill slapped Greg on the shoulder.

"Of course."

The couples were shown to their rooms and said good bye in the hall. As Bill opened the door, a small, white fluff ball barked up at Norma.

"Maf!" tears welled in her eyes as she scooped up the dog and held him close. "Maf, you got me Maf!"

"The only wedding present I could think of that would bring you true happiness." Bill leaned over and stroked the dog's ears.

"You're the best. Really." Norma put Maf on the bed and kissed her husband.

"Start packing, Ethel," Bobby grabbed his wife and twirled her around, "we're moving to New York!" She twirled with him for a moment and then pulled away.

"Just like that? You've decided to accept the nomination and what?" Ethel frowned as she rubbed her rounded belly.

"Ethel, I'm free. I gave my notice today and I'm gone. Let's move and make a new start of it in New York." Bobby sat down on the sofa.

"Bob, be realistic, we won't actually live in New York. Once you're Senator you'll need to be here much of the time." Ethel sat next to him and took his hands.

"So don't pack, we'll buy everything new in New York, but we must live there to prove residency or I can't be the senator." Bobby kissed her knuckles, "Besides, we have so many reasons to love New York."

"I doubt it has anything to do with the fact that Jacquelyn is moving there as well, does it?" Ethel leaned back on the sofa and propped her swollen feet on the coffee table.

"I'll admit that is a good thing. I can still see the kids. They really need a man in their lives."

"Do they or does Jackie need one?" Ethel pouted.

"How can you say that? You know I love you, only you. Holy Mary, mother of Jesus, you know how important family is to me. They need their uncle and I'm going to be sure they see me." Bobby stood up and paced the room. "We have plenty of time to establish residency before the election and more important, before the baby comes. We need to head to New York again soon to find a place."

She sighed, "It's all so exhausting. We can't uproot the children; they have school to attend and their friends are all here. Besides, I need the nanny to be with the younger ones. I'm just so tired."

"Okay, so we'll temporarily split the brood. Anyone not in school goes with us and the others stay here. We'll visit on weekends. That'll make it a little quieter for you during the week." Bobby tapped his finger along his cheek. "I hate to split them up though."

"No way I'm splitting them up. I'll go with you to find a house, but then I want to be here as much as possible and you'll just have to travel back and forth when you can. I'm too pregnant and too tired to uproot everyone."

He came over and kissed her lips, "While I don't like the plan, I will agree it makes the most sense. I've got things to tie up this week. Let's go early next week to find a place. I'll get a real estate agent busy in the meantime."

"Perfect. And Bobby, I'm proud of you." Ethel lumbered to her feet and put her arms around him.

"Family tradition, all of us in politics. With Teddy recovered, and making a great showing in Massachusetts, I'll be sure to win New York. Dad would have us take over the United States."

She waved her hand around the room, "All this from bootlegging with Al Capone. It's impressive."

Chapter 24

Lyndon Johnson stood at his favorite meeting place with Clark Gifford. They were overlooking the Potomac River watching the boats pass underneath. Johnson had a cigarette to his lips. He inhaled deeply and blew out several well-formed smoke rings.

"I know that you were told a while back to forget the death threats to Kennedy. Have any more been received?" Johnson turned to Gifford.

"Not from any of my team."

"Good. He resigned and I'm fully backing his run for the senate. It's simple, he's no longer able to go up against organized crime and I'm free to do what I like. I've tapped a good man for the interim and he won't interfere with my needs or arrest people in my employ." Johnson blew another set of smoke rings.

"That's a good enough reason to back him, but why tell me?" Gifford shrugged.

"Because, I need the death threats to resume once he is settled in New York but I want them to look and feel different. He can live for the time being but let's keep him on his toes."

"I'll verify this with Onassis and then I'll agree. You know he's really the one who runs this business." Gifford turned on his heel and walked away.

Pat stormed into Ethel and Bobby's home in D.C. "Where is he?"

Ethel followed Pat as she went from room to room searching.

"Bobby, where is that sorry skunk?"

"He's not here. What is so urgent?" Ethel stopped and grabbed Pat's arm. She was out of breath from chasing her sister-in-law.

"He lied about Jack and I'm going to kill him, personally." Pat stormed back to the den and threw herself on the couch.

"Yes, he lied to me too. I guess Mary told you." Ethel sighed.

"She did." Pat folded her arms like a petulant child.

"I saw Jack when we were in the Hamptons. He's doing well. He doesn't want us to make a big deal about this. He feels silly that the back surgery was such a ruse that now everyone believes he's dead."

"Yes, I can see why. He's lost everything." Pat leaned forward and took a deep breath.

"Jackie is being a real witch about it. Jack's devastated about the kids. She won't let him see them because they've already mourned the loss and they don't need another shock." Ethel shook her head.

Pat thought about that for a second. "I hate to agree with her about anything, but I do understand that one, at least a little bit."

"Jack doesn't think life is worth living and wishes it really was him in that car. Nothing I've said has made any difference to him. He's lost without the kids and family."

Pat got up and headed to the kitchen, Ethel followed her. "Would you like some cookies?"

"You always have comfort food for every occasion." Pat laughed and got the milk from the refrigerator.

"Where is Jack now?"

"He was in the Hamptons the last I heard. I don't know when he'll return here, but I doubt it'll be much longer. You're welcome to stay with us until he shows up." Ethel handed her a plate of fresh chocolate chip cookies.

"Thanks, to both offers. I can't wait to see Jack. I'm still going to kill Bobby."

"I know how you feel. I wasn't thrilled either." Ethel picked up the latest copy of Harper's Bazaar and thumbed through it while Pat devoured the cookies.

"Does Mom know?"

Ethel looked up from the magazine, "No, I don't think John wants her to. It would be too much for her."

"So I have to keep this to myself?"

"Yes, it would be best. Jack is going to try and persuade Mary to live in a safe house. If that happens, it'll be like he's dead and no one will hear from him again. Let's not give Rose false hope and then crush her." Ethel went back to her article.

Pat sat eating her cookie and thinking, "I guess you're right."

Madeleine Brown tapped a slim slippered foot on the tile of the balcony as she waited for her love. At last Johnson opened the door and came into the hotel room at the Omni in D.C. Madeleine turned to face him as the short negligée she wore twirled around her hips, "You're late, again. Really I don't know why I stay to meet you. You're always in a hurry and don't have a decent amount of time to spend with me. So here's the deal, either you plan to stay the night here, or you leave now."

He walked over to her and put his arms around her waist, "Be reasonable, Maddy, you know I have obligations."

"Yes, you have one to me. Either let her know you will be 'working' all night or I'm leaving." Madeleine's ample cleavage nearly spilled from her nightie.

Johnson squeezed one breast and turned to the phone on the night stand. "You win. How can I turn you down in that outfit?"

Jack wandered back to the cell where Duvalier was trying to drink lukewarm milk with his oatmeal. Jack watched his face make several comical contortions as he tried to swallow the thick pasty goo.

Jack held up the bag of donuts and waved it back and forth in front of the cell door. He then held up the steaming hot cup of coffee. Papa Doc rushed to the cell bars and stared with his mouth watering and agape. "What do I have to do to get that?"

"Tell me who Onassis is hiding on his island. I believe it's Howard Hughes, based on the rumors, but I need to know specifics."

Papa Doc hadn't showered in several days and his odor made Jack take a few steps back. Duvalier thought he was withdrawing the offer and hastily spilled his knowledge, "Onassis hired Meyer Lansky, along with Johnny Roselli to kidnap Hughes and take him to the dungeon at Skorpios. Once he was taken, Robert Mayhue acted as his spokesman and business adviser. Of course, Hughes was unaware of everything that was going on, and they used his fortune to funnel dirty money through his businesses to clean it. He is still on the island and the Mormon Mafia is taking care of him."

"I see. Is he crazy?" Jack leaned closer and waved the bag nearer to the bars.

"Not really. He's got a huge problem with germs and anything dirty but he has his mind and is able to make clear decisions." Papa Doc made a grab for the bag and caught it. Jack let him have it and stepped closer to hand him the coffee.

"Here's the deal, we're going to let you go. You will return to Haiti and never tell a soul what you have seen here nor what has happened. If you do, there will be no charges brought against you for kidnapping an agent of the United States, no time in before a jury. There will simply be a sniper shot that you may or may not hear coming for you. Are we clear?"

Papa Doc swallowed hard, "Yes, I will do as you say."

"One more thing. No more voodoo curses on my family."

Duvalier nodded through a mouthful of donut.

"Finish your donuts and we'll get you showered up and a flight home." Jack turned on his heel and left him gulping coffee as two agents took his place.

One of the agents handed him a clipboard with several blank pages on it. "A full confession of what you've done to Bill Walton and Norma Baker must be written out and signed before you can be released. If you don't want to sign the confession we'll simply leave you here, in this abandoned precinct, and you'll die from starvation."

A terrified Papa Doc, the self-proclaimed king of Haiti and most feared man in his small kingdom, sat down slowly on the cot to think about his options. The agents turned to leave, "You have one hour."

Meyer Lansky smiled as he handed the envelope to Hoover. Hoover had been coming out of the Federal Bureau building when Lansky caught up with him. "A friendly warning. Good evening."

Hoover stood for a moment as Lansky disappeared into the night.

He opened the envelope and saw a picture of him and Clyde, dressed in drag going into a club. He pushed that photo to the bottom of the stack and looked at the next one. Here he was painting Clyde's toenails at the Hotel Del Charro in Coronado, California. *How did they get these?* There were other photos just as damning. The last page was a hand written note.

Dear Edgar,
Stop the crack down on organized crime rings or these will be made public. Your career will be ruined. Think of Clyde.
> Your pals,
> Frank Costello
> Meyer Lansky

Hoover gasped as he read the letter through twice. He replaced the entire packet into the envelope, tucked it into his jacket pocket, and headed home.

Jack was heading out of the station house to go grab a bite to eat. "Mr. Lancer?" Stansel met up with him, "Mr. Kennedy has requested your presence at the Hyannis Port home for the weekend. He wants to have a quiet meeting to discuss the plans."

"Thank you. Will you be there as well?" Jack put on his jacket.

"Yes, if we can get our business wrapped up here."

"I guess we'll meet again."

The last guest had left and Aristotle Onassis threw himself into a high backed chair with a full bottle of whiskey at his elbow. He sat thinking while slowly drinking the bottle dry. Maria Callas had laughed at him as she left, "If you can't control her now during the courting phase you'll never be able to."

He tossed back the last of the whiskey in his glass and threw the empty bottle at the fireplace. He missed and the glass shattered all over the marble flooring near the mantle. A servant came running at the noise, saw the mess, and turned around. He was back a few moments later with a broom and dustpan.

Onassis got up and staggered to the bar, grabbed another bottle, and swayed his way out to the garden.

Christina was sitting on a bench with a book on her lap. He walked up to her and slapped her off the bench, "How dare you talk to Jacquelyn in that manner. I don't care what you think about her, she's our ticket into the good graces of the American public and we need her. I won't have you upset her again "

Christina rubbed her smarting cheek, "I won't." She stood up and faced her father. Her anger matching his. She raised her hand to strike him, but he caught it and forced it to her side.

"Don't be a little fool. I could kill you and no one would convict me. Now, do as I say or I'll ship you to Skorpios and leave you there until you've learned some sense."

Christina was silent for a moment, "You're the fool," she whispered, "That bitch doesn't have any sway with them. I've read the papers. They all hate her and think she's a whore. You're the only one who is holding on to this insane dream that the Americans would ever like you. You'd do better to get one of the actresses to marry you. They are the true royalty in America."

Chapter 25

<u>September 12, 1964</u>

When Bill and Norma returned to the hotel there was a message waiting for them.

You are needed at Hyannis Port, at the compound, this weekend as per Robert Kennedy. Please make sure you arrive Friday evening for an early a.m. meeting on Saturday.

Bill read the note to Norma. "Great, now what does he want from us?" Bill shrugged as he wrote out a reply. Norma looked over his shoulder, "Let him know I'm bringing my dog."

Barbara and Gregory came up to the Walton's as they were deep in conversation at the concierge desk. Barbara waited until the couple was finished.

"Do you want to grab a cup of coffee with us? We would like to talk to you about our plans." Gregory asked them when they turned around.

"Sure." Bill took Norma's hand.

They headed to the little café in the hotel lobby. Norma stopped, "I need to let Maf out. I'll be right back."

Bill handed her the key, "I'd offer, but I know you won't hear of it." He kissed her cheek. "See you in a few minutes. I'll catch them up on our weekend plans."

The trio headed to a back table. As they sat down, a waitress came to take orders. They ordered four coffees and a couple of pieces of apple pie with ice cream.

"We've been summoned to Massachusetts." He paused while the waitress set the cups of steaming coffee on the table, "We have no idea what Robert Kennedy would want with us. After all he just resigned as the Attorney General and we have no idea what a campaign for a senator would look like." Bill stirred some cream and sugar into his coffee and then made Norma's.

"I thought you were giving your resignation to the agency." Greg nodded to the sugar as Bill finished with it.

"I haven't been able to do that yet although that is the plan." Bill smiled as he watched Norma come into the restaurant. She spotted them and waved, quickening her pace to join the trio.

"Did I miss anything?" she asked as she sipped her coffee, "Just the way I like it. Thanks."

Bill nodded and kissed her lightly on the lips, "My pleasure."

Greg cleared his throat, "Can that wait?"

They all laughed as the waitress was bringing over the pie. Once they had devoured them, Barbara began, "We want to buy a spread of land and run a ranch. We're thinking that since you mentioned Texas that sounded great to us. I know it's sudden, but" she took Norma's hand, "you're the best friend I've ever had and I don't want to lose you."

"I'd love living near you. I never thought there was a question about us all being together." Norma squeezed her hand and then let go.

"That's what Greg said, but I didn't want to presume." Barbara sipped her coffee to hide her embarrassment.

"So what is the plan?" Bill asked.

"We were thinking since you have other obligations this weekend that we would head out to Wishbone, Texas and take a look around. I've heard there is some great ranch land there and it's close enough to Amarillo without being in the big city." Greg stirred his newly freshened coffee. "It's a small town of about 1,000 people, give or take. Barbara grew up there and says it's got a lot of lovely ranch homes that'll sell for a song."

"I agree that the price will be lower in a small town of that size. I can start with that." Bill agreed. "As soon as our weekend obligations are over, I'll go to the agency on Monday and see what I need to do to resign and get my full benefits."

Barbara and Norma clapped in unison. Norma choked on her tears, "A real life at last."

Bill placed his arm around her shoulders, "Yes love, a real life at last."

Papa Doc finished his shower and got dressed in the clothes the agents brought him from his vehicle. As he was tucking the last of his things in the suitcase an agent came to get him.

"There is one last thing you have to do before you can leave." Latimer told him.

Duvalier looked up at him with trepidation.

"You must pay restitution to the diner that was wrecked while we were trying to rescue Walton and Baker. Here is the bill."

Latimer handed him an itemized bill.

"Wait a minute here, I don't owe you for 'rounds fired during the encounter'." Papa Doc read the list.

"Okay, I'll take you back to the cell. What's a few bucks for shells in comparison to dying of hunger in a prison cell?" Latimer took out a set of handcuffs, "But it is your choice, and if this is how you want to die, who am I to question it?"

"I'll pay it. Don't be so hasty." Papa Doc opened up the wallet they had returned to him. "I don't have that much cash on me."

"That's too bad, now isn't it? You see the U.S. government doesn't trust you to make good on the debt."

"Send a wire to Louis DeJoie and he can take care of it." Duvalier wrote down his instructions to the Senatuer and handed it to Latimer.

"Okay, I'll let you wait in the conference room, but if he doesn't answer, it's back to the cell until this debt is resolved."

Papa Doc sighed and followed the agent to the empty room. He sat at the big oval table. Latimer summoned Stansel who stood outside the door playing guard until Latimer got the required answer.

Khrushchev listened as the angry mob grew closer to the Kremlin. They had begun chanting and causing chaos a few days earlier. He turned to his aide, "How long do you think they will keep this up?"

"It is rumored that you must be overthrown and someone who sympathizes with Castro will be put in your place." The aide shrugged, "I'm not surprised about the sentiment but I agree that nuclear war is not anything any nation can win at."

"Isn't there anyway to stop these mad men?" Khrushchev coughed.

"No, the moment you lost face with the world, and made Castro look a-fool, and over the Cuban Missile Crises, you sealed your fate. These people are not all

Russian, many have been sent on Castor's orders. The rioting is Castro's influence here in the Soviet Union as well. From the intel we've gathered, we can just about guarantee that they are from the mafia."

Ethel watched Bobby pack his suitcase. "Where to this time?"

"I'm off to the compound." Bobby turned to look at her, t-shirt in hand.

"You're going to see your folks and didn't tell me?" Ethel looked hurt.

"No, I'm going to a meeting for the weekend. It'll be boring. I've taken the liberty of making sure the meeting is in the clubhouse and we'll be staying in the guest houses off the property.

"That means Jack will be there and you don't want your mother to see him." Ethel folded her arms and tapped her foot, "Robert Francis Kennedy, what are you up to now?"

Duvalier was led from his comfy chair back to the cell. Latimer refused to discuss the issue until the door was securely locked behind him. "DeJoie informs me that you do not have enough money to pay this debt. I would suggest you write him a note, tell him where your personal stash is, and have him hand the full sum to the courier we will dispatch to handle this matter. Of course, you will have to pay the fee for the courier and the gasoline required to fuel the jet to take him to Haiti and back."

"This is the limit!" Duvalier shouted.

"Yes, and you are guilty of kidnapping a government employee of the United States of America." Latimer shrugged as he pushed a pen and paper through the bars. "I'll wait."

Papa Doc snubbed the items and let them fall to the floor.

"You have fifteen minutes. If you don't comply we're locking up and leaving." Latimer turned with a grin on his face. "You're not so tough now are you, prince or president or whatever stupid title you've given yourself."

Jacquelyn finally found a home she liked and put in an offer. She went back to the hotel where Caroline and John-John were waiting.

"I've found us a home. Let's just hope that the owners accept our offer."

"I don't want to move here." Caroline whined as tears welled in her eyes.

"But Uncle Bobby is moving here too. We'll all be together." Jackie knelt down to her daughter's level. "That will be nice, won't it?"

"No. Why can't we all stay where we are? I have friends there. I don't want to leave them." Caroline complained as John-John joined in.

"I don't want to either. I like my school."

"Look, this is what Mommy needs and I'm sorry you don't like it, but you will adjust to the new house, new school, and you'll make new friends. We need to be away from the hateful people in D.C." Jackie stood up and headed to the kitchen. "Now, I'll hear no more about this. Let's have dinner."

"I'm not hungry." Caroline turned away from her mother.

"Me either." John-John followed his sister out of the room to their private bedroom in the hotel suite.

Why must everything I want be so difficult? Jackie went to the wet bar and took out a bottle of wine. She poured herself a large goblet and settled on the balcony. *No one cares about my needs or my desires. It's always all about everyone else.*

Hoover sat in the office of the acting Attorney General, waiting on the man to end his phone conversation.

Finally, he replaced the receiver on the hook, "I'm sorry about that, Mr. Hoover. To what do I owe this pleasure?"

"I just wanted to see what direction you were planning on taking as A.G."

Nicholas Katzenbach smiled a little, "As I'm only the acting A.G., I've decided to just do the minimum and see what needs to be handled. Johnson wants me to be more involved with his campaign than anything else right now. I've determined to focus my energy on finding out dirt on Nixon. He looks like a crook, so this shouldn't be a difficult task."

"Sounds prudent to me. The President must come first." Hoover mentally sighed in relief as he left the office.

"The courier has returned. We asked him to get you enough money for the return trip home. Basically, DeJoie was a little reluctant to help you out. It seems the country is doing fine without you." Latimer chuckled as Duvalier threw his coffee cup across the cell. It shattered against the bars.

Stansel shook his head, "Tsk tsk. What a temper. It's too bad he didn't allow you to finish."

Duvalier watched the agents laughing at him. "Well, am I free or not?"

"Actually you are. We've scheduled you on the next freighter out of New York. It leaves at two a.m." Latimer continued to laugh.

"What? The President of Haiti cannot ride on a freighter ship. I demand better transportation."

"Well, you didn't give clear instructions and DeJoie didn't want his head to end up on a pike for disobeying you. This was the cheapest way to send you back to a poverty stricken nation. For one, I believe that you keep in poverty due to your misappropriations of funds. The United States government has given you a good bit of money. You have failed to use it as per our agreement. What you have been required to repay as damages here, is just a drop in the bucket." Latimer opened the door and Stansel handed Duvalier a broom and dustpan he had retrieved from a corner.

"Clean that up and you'll be escorted to the docks."

Cole Porter sat with Truman Capote as the play ended, "Well done, my friend. It is one of your better efforts. I'm almost tempted to write you a score on this piece." Cole patted him on the back.

"Thanks, this one was easier to write. I think I'm getting better with every play."

"No doubt." Porter stood up on the first row with Capote.

They watched as Hoover and Clyde Tolson stood up and prepared to go back stage. Ella Fitzgerald was with them. She entered the aisle and led the way to the stage doors on the left.

Truman began to chuckle, "You know that there are rumors flying around about those two. I hear they are more than friends and co-workers."

"Do tell? I've seen them at some of the drag parties but I never would have put them together as a couple."

"I believe it's true."

"What proof do you have?" Porter watched them as they left the audience area and went back stage.

"I overheard one of Giancana's men say they have photos of them together in a hotel room."

"Doing what?"

"Look Porter, the likes of you doesn't need to ask 'doing what?' I'm sure you know full well what." Truman chuckled as he headed out the aisle and back stage.

"Let's go find them and make them sweat a little. It is my favorite past time." Truman laughed heartily.

Chapter 26

<u>September 14, 1964</u>

Jack Lancer watched as Mary Meyer got out of the car at the compound. He ran to her, "Mary! I had no idea you'd be here." He threw his arms around her and twirled her around a few times before setting her back on her feet and kissing her soundly.

She grinned as she caught her breath, "It's good to see you too, Jack."

"Do you know why you're here?"

"I would imagine the diary." Mary followed him up the walkway to the house.

"Of course."

Mary grabbed his hand as they started up the steps to the porch, "Who all has been summoned?"

"That's a great word, 'summoned'. I know that Ethel insisted on being here but I'm not really certain who else aside from Bill Walton and Norma Baker." Jack waited for the footman to open the front door for them.

"I don't know them, do I?" Mary wrinkled her brow.

"No, they've been out of the country." Jack kept the explanation brief. "Do you want to stay in my room? I've got a king sized bed."

She leaned closer to him, "Yes, I'd love too. I've missed you. Will anyone mind?"

"Mind? Why would they mind? Besides, I'm part owner of this place." Jack stopped in the middle of the entry hall. "I guess I'm not any longer."

"Come on Jack, it's alright. We'll figure it out."

"Will we? I'm legally dead. I don't have any form of income, no way to support us and nowhere to live. And to top it all off, there are people who want you dead because of your diary and what you know. What kind of life could we have?"

"Let's go to your room and talk about it in private." Mary nodded to the porter to follow them with her bag. "We'll be fine, really. Bobby will help us sort it all out."

Ethel and Bobby arrived later that afternoon in Hyannis Port. They took a limo to the big house to see Rose and Joe. Ethel stepped out of the car with the help of her husband.

The door was thrown open as Rose came out to greet them. She was dressed, as what can only be described as an Indian maiden. On her feet she wore a pair of moccasins. She had a head band around her forehead with one feather sticking up on the right side above her ear.

Ethel held a hand over her mouth to stifle the laughter that bubbled up at this site.

Rose came down the steps and hugged her son.

"Hello Mom," Bobby sneezed as the feather had been tickling his nose. "It's good to see you.

"Bobby, you're looking well. Ethel, how are you?" Rose turned to greet her daughter-in-law. She hugged her for a second and moved back to Bobby.

"I'm well." Ethel responded, "How are you doing, Rose? It's been a while since we've seen you."

"I'm good. I was just playing cowboys and Indians with the neighbor kids. They keep me young." Rose took off the headband and smiled down at her shoes, "I have to say these are really comfortable. I hate to give them back to Ilene."

"Maybe I'll get you a pair for Christmas, Mom." Bobby followed her back into the house.

The children were sitting in the middle of the foyer, legs crossed Indian style. "Go home now, children." Rose commanded.

They got up and got ready to leave, "Can I have my shoes, Ms. Rose?" Ilene asked in a shy voice.

Rose held up first one foot then the other as the child removed them for her.

"Thank you." Ilene and her siblings left the house.

"Now," Rose turned to her own children, "what's going on?"

"We needed a quiet place to strategize and this was the only place I could think of to do it. I've got to get a campaign plan figured out. So we'll visit with you this evening and check in on Dad, but tomorrow, we will be in the guest houses and probably won't see you again."

"Oh yes you will. I won't be left out of your discussions. I know a thing or two about politics and I can offer up advice."

As Rose led the way into the living room, Ethel whispered, "It figures. She's in her right mind just when we need her to be out of it."

As Jack led Mary to the guest club house, they saw Norma and Bill heading through the doors. Bobby and Ethel could be seen standing in the foyer awaiting everyone.

Bobby was talking intently with Stansel as Jack and Mary came into the building. Ethel hugged them both and pointed them to the ballroom.

"Everyone is here." Ethel nudged Bobby.

"Let's go." Bobby and Rex Stansel walked together to the large round table set up in a corner of the room. Everyone was seated and waiting on them.

"Good morning everyone." Bobby began as Stansel found a seat. Bobby headed to the chalkboard leaning on a large easel and picked up the chalk. "This will be an informal meeting and the purpose is a game plan for thwarting LBJ and Onassis in their collective endeavors."

Everyone nodded at him, Bill stood up, "I would like to say something before we get too far into this thing."

Bobby smiled and waited, "The floor is yours, Mr. Walton."

"I've decided to retire from the agency. While that is exciting news," Bill looked down to Norma and pulled her up by the elbow, "our marriage is certainly the most exciting news to date."

Ethel squealed and rushed to hug Norma. Congratulations were given along with pats on the back and lots of hugging. Norma actually blushed, "Thank you."

"I can't believe it. This is the greatest news ever," Ethel gushed, "I had so hoped you would find happiness."

"Oh Ethel, you're the one who saved me from a life of hiding. Thank you for giving me hope that I could have a life. Bill and I are going to move to Texas and start an acting school." Norma fairly glowed as she told the group of the plans they had made, "Oh and Barbara, you know, Nurse Hadley, married Gregory Morris and they are moving to Texas with us. It'll all work out so perfectly."

Bobby stepped forward and hugged her, "I'm happy for you Norma."

"Bill got me Maf back!" Norma laughed. I would bring him to the meeting but Bill said I needed to leave him in the room."

Bobby shook his head, "No you don't. Five-minute break while Norma goes to get her dog. There's a continental breakfast set up behind Latimer."

Chapter 27

Latimer swallowed a bit of donut with a sheepish grin. Bobby grinned, "I see he's already found the refreshments."

Everyone laughed and relaxed as Norma returned with Maf. A cute, white fluff ball practically jumping from her arms.

Mary came over to Norma, "Hi there, I don't think we've ever been properly introduced. I'm Mary Meyer."

Norma held out her empty hand, "Norma Baker, I mean Walton."

"Yes, I know who you are. I just wanted to thank you for taking care of Jack when he first had to deal with his situation. You've helped him deal with losing everything. He told me who you really are. Don't worry, your secret is safe with me."

"Mary, you don't need to thank me. I do know how hard it is to adjust to a new life. I also appreciate your confidence and hope we can be friends." Norma gave her a warm smile as everyone began to find their seats again. Once she was settled, Maf laid down on her lap and went to sleep as she stroked his back.

Bobby stood in front of the chalkboard with a piece of chalk. He wrote 'LBJ' on one side and 'Onassis' on the other side, and then drew a line down the middle.

"Now, who has any information that we can use against these men?"

"I have a ton of notes in my diary, Ethel. Did you bring it?" Mary Meyer looked over to her friend.

"I've hidden it. No one will be able to find it." Ethel shrugged. "I also received the letter you sent and it's with the diary in a safe place."

"It's best. I know the FBI and CIA are both following me around, and the CIA wants me dead. They know that I researched everything about Jack, including the bullet that came through the front windshield striking him in the neck, and how he was shot in the *back* of the head from the book depository. I came to the conclusion, in my numerous scenarios and drawings, that there had to have been at least two shooters. One was Johnny Roselli for certain and the other one was more than likely Eugene Brady. Fratianno was the lookout for Roselli, who was hired by Johnson, but it was Clark Gifford who went to Roselli for Johnson." Mary paused to take a drink of her orange juice. "I think that's about it."

"What about Oswald?" Latimer asked.

"He made the shot that took off the back of the scalp, but he was only a dupe. His real beef was with Connelly, but someone else, probably Roselli, shot the President first. I believe that Roselli thought Jack was in the first car and realized his mistake too late. As the car carrying the President approached, he had time to aim and take the shot that went through Jack's neck."

"I can certainly see why you've made yourself some enemies. What about Cord?" Bill asked, "Everyone knows he's dirty. He works both sides and will do anything that makes him more powerful."

"Cord is an informant for Onassis."

Bobby jotted that down on the board under Onassis. "Anything else? What about LBJ?"

"He's been having an affair with Madeleine Brown for over twenty years. Lady Bird knows about her. Madeleine told me he has a reputation for doing business with Onassis. They are trying to run munitions to Vietnam to escalate the conflict into a full blown war by providing weapons to both sides. According to his mistress, LBJ orchestrated, at least in part, the assassination because he had been 'snubbed one too many times'." Mary took a deep breath, and sipped her orange juice as she leaned back in her chair.

Bobby looked at Mary, "Do you have any proof?"

"Yes, his mistress told me herself. She told me a few weeks after the assassination that the night before Jack was shot that Johnson told her, 'After tomorrow those damned Kennedys are never going to embarrass me again. That's not a threat; that's a promise'."

"I knew it!" Jack jumped to his feet, "That slimy bastard! He was so mad about my moving the troops out of Vietnam. It's also all about image and money and power. He didn't have the image or power but by damned he'll manage to get money off of this conflict one way or another." Jack slammed a fist into the wall and shook it as the pain registered. Maf barked at the sudden noise and everyone laughed as the tension broke.

Latimer looked at Mary who was still watching Jack with concern. "So, Mary, how do you know so much about all of this?"

"Cord kept detailed notes for the CIA and I read them. He also noted that the CIA had been ordered to stand down if shots were fired, that's why they were so slow to protect the motorcade. It was Johnson's idea to leave the tops down for the ride. He wanted all of his fellow Texans to be able to clearly see him. Jacquelyn agreed because she hadn't had time to get her hair done." Mary answered with confidence.

Bobby shook his head as he wrote on the LBJ side, "CIA, direct threat, munitions."

Stansel had been silent, listening, taking notes and absorbing. "I have a question for Ms. Meyer. How do you know all of this is fact?"

"Oh, Madeleine and I have been friends for decades. All women love to gossip and she's no different, especially when she believes I'm her confidante, and I was too, until she informed me it was LBJ who wanted Jack dead. That ended our friendship." Mary sighed, "Can someone else talk for a while? I've unloaded everything I know."

Norma piped up, "I can tell you what happened when Bill and I were kidnapped by Duvalier."

All eyes swung to Norma. "Go ahead." Bobby nodded to her.

"He wanted to know where Jack Kennedy was. He had seen us when we were in a dance troupe with Maria Callas in Paris. The whole point of that was to help Jack adjust to his new life and see if we could get information about Onassis from Maria. I found out that Onassis was the one who ordered my death. Papa Doc was almost certain I was on stage, but when he saw Jacquelyn Kennedy's face when Jack danced close to the edge of the stage, he knew that John was there as well."

Bobby jotted down Marilyn's death under Onassis.

Norma stroked Maf and continued, "Then he was on a mission to prove we were both still alive and that Onassis' plans had failed. He drugged Jacquelyn with a truth serum and she told Papa Doc John was still alive, but she didn't know where he was. She also told Onassis he was alive, as well as Lee and her shrink and anyone who would listen; but of course no one believed her but Papa Doc.

"After he finished with her he had his spies find out where I was. By this time I had returned to the U.S. and was with Barbara. He then planned the kidnapping in the park but he didn't plan on Bill coming with me." She reached over and patted Bill's arm. "My hero."

"Anytime, doll face." Bill told her in his best Bugsy imitation. Everyone laughed while Bobby wrote 'truth serum' to the added Papa Doc category near the bottom of the chalk board.

"When we finally were captured, Duvalier came to us and tortured me. He wanted me to confess that I was Marilyn Monroe. For several hours I denied it and insisted I was Norma Baker but he threatened, 'I'll throw acid in your beautiful face. That way no one would ever want you again.'

"Bill begged me to tell him I was Marilyn Monroe." Norma stopped for the dramatic effect.

There was a collective gasp and they all leaned forward as she finished, "I told him what he wanted to hear and then he claimed I was lying. I assured him I wasn't and he finally calmed down. He left the shack screaming 'I knew it'!"

Everyone was still until Bill broke the silence, "I wanted to kill the bastard, but he had me tied to a chair, half drugged, and I was defenseless. While he didn't strike me he caused me great mental anguish. I was watching the woman I loved get smacked around like a punching bag. I still want to kill that son of a bitch."

"Well, you helped me learn some tricks of the agency and we made it out, together. That's all that matters to me." Norma put her hand in his. He pulled it up to his lips and kissed her hand.

"I will tell you that when I was kidnapped and being held on Skorpios, I met Howard Hughes. Did you know he's been a prisoner there for years? The Morman Mafia have taken over his business and Maheu has been his acting manager and business consultant. Let me tell you, they never consult him and his businesses are being used to funnel dirty money."

Jack turned to her, "I've heard that just recently. Is he still there?"

"Yes, he was still there when Barbara rescued me. She got to me before Papa Doc and Onassis could really do any real damage to me." Marilyn shuttered at the memory.

Bobby looked at Jack, "There's your next mission. You and Latimer need to somehow arrange to bring him back to the states. It's not my call anymore because I've resigned, but I'm sure it'll be top priority once the director learns of it."

Latimer grimaced, "I just want to spend a few weeks here in the states doing nothing but watching the yard grow. Won't this wait?"

"I don't really think it will. Once we have Jack reveal himself to LBJ, it may be too late. This is priority." Bobby insisted.

"Back to Onassis real quick," Jack stopped the discussion, "He and LBJ, along with Walter Jenkins and Margaret Smith, want to control the Saudi Arabia oil shipments to the U.S. They plan to siphon money off of a lucrative arms and munitions contract that will name them exclusively as providers of weapons for the 'Golden Triangle', which consists of Vietnam, Cambodia, and Laos. You may have already gleaned all of this but they plan to get a shipping dock set up in New Hampshire where they can run their 'businesses' without much interference."

Bobby jotted down Golden Triangle – munitions on both LBJ and Onassis sides and then circled them together.

"Excellent information we're getting here." Bobby smiled as he looked around the room. He was turning back to the chalkboard when Rose walked in with a tea tray.

Chapter 28

"Would anyone care for a fresh cup of tea? Sometimes coffee is just too much at these things." She came closer to the table and spotted Norma. She smiled at her as she placed the tray on the table next to Stansel's elbow, "Good morning, why aren't you with the children?"

Norma smiled back, "Good morning. I got married. I'm no longer employed by Robert and Ethel."

"Congratulations dear, you deserve to have your own children. Is this your husband?" Rose walked over to Bill and shook his hand.

Norma nodded as Rose greeted Bill, "You take good care of this lady, young man. She saved Mary Kerry from being kidnapped after the funeral for my poor John."

"I will, Ma'am. You have nothing to worry about." Bill smiled as Jack ducked lower in his chair.

Jack caught Bobby's eye and they both had the same panicked expression. Ethel stood up, "Rose, let me help you with that tray."

"Jack, my poor dear son. This family has mourned him so. My dear husband has never gotten over the loss." Rose wiped away a tear as she turned to Ethel. "Thank you, dear."

"Let me help you back to the house, Rose. It's sometimes a bit overwhelming to think of our loss." Ethel winked at Jack as she led Rose out of the room.

Stansel sat with his mouth open for a moment, "She doesn't know? How unusual."

"No, it would just cause her more grief later. I can't be who I was and who I am is pathetic at best. It's better this way. Besides, the fewer people who know who I am the better it is." Jack sat up straight and took a shaky sip of his coffee.

"If you think so." Stansel didn't sound convinced. "It's my turn to tell what I know. I know that Christian called the precinct before we left to inform me that Onassis had bought a 'ridiculously large ring' for Mrs., er, Jacqueline Kennedy. He also said that Christina came to the study with a large bruise across her face. When he asked about it, she said it was nothing and he needed to mind his own business." Stansel shook his head, "That child deserved whatever she got. Christian says she is something else. She has agreed to be nicer to the 'witch' in the future. So apparently, Onassis is going to try the 'more flies with honey' bit on Jacquelyn."

Bobby wrote 'engagement?' on the board. He sighed, "I hate that bastard. We need to do whatever we can in order to keep him from gaining any business or support what-so-ever in this country."

Jack spoke up, "So how are we going to keep him from getting in here?"

Bobby looked around the group, "We will divide the duties up. Everyone will have a specific goal and how that is accomplished will be up to you."

Ethel returned from taking Rose to the house. "She's almost certain that John was here. I tried to convince her that she was just having an 'off' day today." Ethel sat down, "She is wearing me out."

"Good job, honey." Bobby walked over to her and kissed her on the top of her head. "Do you think you convinced her that it wasn't Jack?"

"I don't think entirely." Ethel shook her head, "I expect her to come back in here at some point today."

"We're almost finished. Jack, you can go after your assignment is given out." Bobby returned to the chalkboard.

"The last thing we need is for Mom to figure it out."

"Actually, you're in charge of convincing LBJ to back off of the Vietnam conflict. He needs to rethink the munitions and selling to both sides. Let him know you're on to him. You'll know what to do. Also mention to him that we are aware of Onassis' 'Turkish cigarettes' and he can't have a dock in McIntrye's state. We don't need an open market on opium here." Bobby jotted 'opium' on the chalkboard.

"I've got it. I'm out of here. Come on Mary." Jack stood up and Mary followed suit.

Bobby turned to them, "Mary, I want you to go to a safe house. Your detail may not always be able to protect you and now that I've resigned I can't guarantee how long they will actually be assigned to you."

"I'll think about it." Mary agreed and the couple left out the back way.

"Latimer, I can't let Jack go with you to rescue Howard Hughes. Maybe you could get the director to send someone with you to go and get him. I know you don't want to go, but Norma can give you the details on where he is."

"I will be in contact with Prince Saud and Prince Rainier to call in favors. They won't do business with Onassis if I ask them not to. That will keep him from getting a few things he wants even though it won't really help here."

"Stansel, I want you to find out who his mob cronies are here in the states and go at them. I know Sam Giancana is one of them."

"Got it."

"Okay, I guess that's it. Norma and Bill, congratulations on your new life. May God Bless you and keep you safe. You know you can always contact me or Ethel if you'd like."

Norma got up and hugged Bobby and then Ethel. Stansel and Latimer took their cue and stood up as well.

"Thank you for everything," Norma hugged the men and Bill shook hands all around. "If you're ever in Texas, look us up."

Lee answered her telephone on the second ring, "Hello?"

"Lee? It's me." Jackie breathed into the phone on her bedroom night stand, "I've just found out that Truman Capote has been spreading rumors about us. He's telling whoever will listen that you were sleeping with Jack."

"But, I was while you were off with Bill Holden." Lee sighed and lit a cigarette. "The past is past and this entire conversation is tiresome. He's going to do whatever he wants. Just roll with it and laugh it off."

"Lee, you know I can't do that. My kids will find out and what will Caroline think? She's at that tender age, asking about mommies and daddies; nothing sexual, but still asking about Onassis and if we're going to be mommy and daddy to her and John-John. She'll understand this stuff soon enough."

"Jacks, you worry too much. Have you seen Dr. Feel Good lately? He could help you out."

"I don't know why I even bother with you. Does nothing ever faze you?" Jackie sighed.

"Not very much. I keep in close contact with the good doctor, I highly recommend that you do as well."

Jackie sighed and hung up the phone. As she turned to go back into the living room she was stopped short by Ari. "Where've you been hiding?"

Jackie nearly jumped at his sudden appearance. "I've just been looking for my magazine on my night stand. I've not been hiding."

Ari smiled and pulled her into his arms, "Sometimes I think you're avoiding me."

She twisted her head upwards to look into his eyes, "Sometimes, you are correct."

He managed a constrained laugh, "My little feisty bella." He kissed her forehead and let her go. "I've been thinking about what you said to me about John still being alive. I would like to hear more about that."

"Are you saying that you believe me?" Jackie looked relieved.

"I'm saying it's possible that I believe you. Why don't we go have a little drink, and you can tell me all about it." Ari led her back down the hallway and into the den. He walked over to the decanter and poured them both a shot of whiskey. He added a little seltzer water to hers, watering it down a bit and handed her the glass.

Chapter 29

September 20, 1964

Aristotle sat on his yacht drinking with Sam Giancana. He was still docked in the harbor in New York. Sam finished his drink and poured himself another glass.

Onassis waited until Sam finished topping off his glass, "When will Khrushchev be ousted?"

"It's hard to tell. He knows he's going to be overthrown and that fact is keeping him out of the country. If he doesn't return soon I'll arrange to have him called back on an emergency. Then we'll be able to get him out."

Onassis nodded, "I'm growing impatient. I want him out before the end of the year. Though sooner would be better."

Johnson listened as Jenkins laid out the latest. He handed Johnson a hefty envelope stuffed with money. "Here is your payout on the two submarines. I've sent Onassis his in untraceable bills through a currier to

New York. He signed for it this morning. McIntrye and Smith have also been paid."

"Thank you, Walter. I appreciate you."

"Of course, there was a great deal of talk at the Pentagon about where so much money had walked off too. Maybe we should back away for a little while and let the heat die down."

"Like hell we will. The war needs to actually be a war and my munitions agreement with Onassis needs to be fulfilled in the next few months or I'll be out millions of dollars in profit. We will push through this Jenkins, and I know you will be able to get the job done."

"Lyndon, I've been with you a long time. I'll do what you ask, but it'll be at the risk of getting caught. If that happens, I don't know anything about any of it. You'll hang on your own for your hasty actions." Jenkins left Johnson fuming.

Georgi waited on Marita to come out of her room. She had been there for several weeks now and their friendship had grown.

Marita opened the door and saw him standing there, she smiled, "Good morning."

He took her arm and led her down the hallway, "I just wanted to let you know that your presence here makes my life bearable."

"Why thanks, Georgi, you do the same for me. I guess we're stuck here for life."

"Yes, unless you want to do some facial surgery to change your looks. I personally think that would be a tragedy." He smiled and held out her chair. He pushed it in as she sat down.

"I don't think I'd ever want to do that. I hate pain." She laughed as Alice appeared in the doorway. "Morning Alice."

"Good morning. Would you like your usual?"

"Yes, please." They chimed together.

"It's good to see you happy, Georgi." Alice turned back to the kitchen and left them alone.

"Well, you know that old question about if you had to be stranded on a deserted island with someone who would you pick?" Marita asked

He nodded as he poured himself some coffee. He held up a mug and she agreed. "I'd probably choose you."

He grinned as he handed her the cup.

Castro was relaxing in his chair when his aide came in. "I brought you the latest data on the sugar deal." He handed a sheaf of papers to Ficel.

Castro looked it over and smiled, "Good. This is good!"

The aide stood where he was for a moment. Castro waved him away, "Out."

The aide bowed before the dictator and left the room. Castro got up and walked over to the phone. He dialed a number and waited through a series of beeps as the international call was connected. The phone rang on the other end a couple of times before it was picked up.

"Angelton?"

"Speaking."

"I need you to get a message to Onassis." Castro barked into the receiver. "Tell him that the deal is going well but I still need that Russian asshole ousted so I can move on the nuke deal."

"I'll tell him." Angelton hung up the phone.

Castro leaned back in the huge leather chair and lit a cigar.

Jackie was instructing the movers on what furniture needed to be moved to New York when Johnson suddenly appeared on her doorstep.

She saw him, "Mr. President, what a surprise!" She seemed a little nervous.

He stepped into the room and surveyed the goings on. "I see the move is progressing. You weren't trying to avoid having to tell me good-bye, were you?"

"I don't understand why that would be necessary. There is no reason for me to explain to you my whereabouts." She stood up taller.

"No reason at all, I just thought it would be the polite thing for you to do. After all, we do have a history." He moved a little closer and looked as though he wanted to embrace her. She took a few steps away and tidied a stack of newspapers.

"I was going to send you and Lady Bird a nice note." Jackie turned her back to him.

"That really won't do. What I would prefer is a hug, at least." Johnson came close to her again.

"I'm sorry about that, but I'm really busy now. I can't stop for long. Not even for you, Mr. President."

"Don't play coy with me, Jackie, you know you've had a thing for me for a while. I don't understand why you sent Robert to threaten me." Johnson looked hurt and stuck out his bottom lip.

"I didn't send him, he just went. I don't like you, in that manner, and would appreciate it if you'd leave me to finish my packing." Jackie moved aside so the movers could take the couch out of the house, effectively removing the obstacle in his way.

"I know you like older, powerful men with lots of money. I happen to fit that description."

"You do, but I'm not at liberty to really care for a married man. I must go now. Have a good life." Jackie hurried out of the room and left him standing alone with the movers.

Fuming at the rebuff, Johnson turned on his heel and stormed out the front door. Jackie watched from the kitchen and nearly cried in relief when he actually left the house.

Caroline came in search of her mother, "Why was the big scary man here?"

"It's all right. He's gone now." Jackie hugged her daughter to her for a moment. "He is one of the reasons we need to move to New York."

Bobby and Ethel returned to the main house. Bobby was carrying the tea tray that Rose had brought down earlier.

Ethel sighed, "I'm beat. That was a lot of information being thrown about for such a short meeting. I'm so happy for Norma, though. Bill is a good man."

"Yes, although I know you'll miss her." Bobby walked alongside his wife.

"I will, but we can always talk on the phone some and write letters." She patted her round belly, "I hope they decide to have kids. She's nearing the age where she won't be able to soon."

Bobby thought for a moment, "They can always adopt."

"It's a shame she can't get her hands on her own estate. She could get everything back, including her money to help them start off." Ethel stopped to allow Bobby to open the front door for her.

"He's got plenty. Don't you worry about them." Bobby answered as they walked into the foyer. "MOTHER, where are you?"

"In the living room. Is that you Bobby?"

"Yes, Mother."

"Do you have that nice Nelly with you? I'm so glad you married her instead of that frumpy Ethel." Rose smiled at them as they came into the living area.

Bobby placed his arm around Ethel, more for the moral support than out of necessity. "Me too, Mother." He smiled down at Ethel and kissed her cheek. "This lady is all I need."

Ethel returned his smile and breathed a sigh of relief. Rose had turned to the plate of cookies on the coffee table in front of her, "At least she won't remember this morning."

"True." Bobby helped her into a chair across from Rose and put the tray down on the end table.

"Did you bring John with you?" Rose asked.

"Holy Mother of God." Bobby whispered under his breath. "No, Mom." Bobby walked over to Rose and sat down next to her on the couch. "You know he was killed a year ago, remember?" He gently patted her shoulder as he spoke.

"That's what I thought too, but I know I saw him today." Rose insisted.

"The man you saw today was his old body double." Bobby looked over to Ethel, "We never should have brought him to the meeting. It's too upsetting for Mother."

"I'm sorry, Rose," Ethel agreed, "We never should have allowed him here. We just weren't thinking." Ethel hung her head in remorse.

"It wasn't his double. It was John. I'll know it until my dying day. I'm sure you have a good reason for lying to me, but I'll have you know that I KNOW!"

Chapter 30

<u>September 28, 1964</u>

Norma and Barbara were looking at properties around Wishbone, Texas with their hubbies. They finally settled on a large spread with sixty acres and decided to turn the ranch hands house into a little home for Barbara and Greg.

Norma danced around Bill in excitement. "I can't believe this is ours. We're going to live here and ranch. What are we going to ranch?"

Bill laughed as he caught her hand and pulled her to him. "I think that we can all decide that once we find ourselves one of those famed Texas steaks and a big baked potato. Come on, let's celebrate."

Barbara and Greg agreed. Greg opened the screen door for the group, "The contractor said it would only take a couple of weeks to transform our little home. If we look at the realistic statistics, it should be more like two months. Do you think you can stand us in your guest room for that long?"

Bill turned to the couple, "Of course! We wouldn't have it any other way. Welcome home!"

Howard Hughes got off the private jet in Las Vegas with Maheu and several other members of the Mormon Mafia. They stepped into a limo and sped away to the Dessert Inn.

"I want some banana nut ice cream from Baskin Robbins." Hughes demanded. "I haven't had great ice cream in forever."

"I'll make sure you get some." Maheu told him as they swept him past the hotel desk clerk and into the elevator. They whizzed to the top floor. "Here is your suite. We hope you'll like it here." Maheu left a man at the door as he left. "I'll take care of your luggage and bring you some ice cream."

Jim Angelton watched as Cord Meyer crossed the street to get a newspaper from the stand on the corner. After a moment, Cord came back to the coffee shop on the side of the street where Angelton was waiting.

Cord opened the door to the little café and went in with Jim on his heels. Cord turned suddenly and caught Angelton by the neck. He dropped his hand as soon as he recognized Jim's face.

"You're quick," Angelton reached up and rubbed his throat.

"Sorry about that. You shouldn't follow a man that closely." Cord moved out of the way of incoming foot traffic.

"If I don't follow you this closely I'll never find you. You've done a great job of avoiding me for over two weeks now." Jim found a seat and motioned for Cord to sit down.

"Look Jim, we both know that I'm not going to turn Mary over to you. And her diary or whatever the hell it is you think you want, just can't be found. You're the mole everyone is looking for, of that I'm sure. We may be in

Onassis' back pocket, but a mole is a huge black stain on your reputation to say the least. I'm sure others know about it, but I doubt the right people do. Yes, I'm a dirty creep, but at least I have some sense of loyalty. Mary isn't going to say or do anything with that diary and you should let this go."

"So," Jim took a moment to stare at Cord, "you're not going to help and you want us to leave poor old Mary alone. After all, she's just one lady and what can she do to damage anything? Is that it?"

Cord watched Jim, but held his tongue. Jim continued, "Let me tell you what you apparently are to fucking stupid to grasp. She can ruin everything, not only for Onassis, but also for Johnson. Not to mention the damage to the CIA. We all need her to keep silent. The only way to ensure that is to kill her. Dead people do not talk."

Cord shook his head, "I don't want to have to turn you in as a mole, Angelton, but I will in order to stop this nonsense. I tell you, Mary isn't a threat."

Jim just got up, "Do what you feel you must, but she will be silenced." He walked away leaving Cord frantically trying to figure out the next move.

Lyndon Johnson was sitting behind his desk in the Oval Office when the French doors opened from outside. He turned sharply to see the figure of a tall man coming in past the hanging sheers. "I used to love slipping out through these doors and playing with John-John," Jack stated as he came into the office and took a seat opposite the President. "He used to play under that desk, right there. He loved playing horsey on my foot while I was trying to work.

Johnson stared at John Kennedy aka Jack Lancer for a full minute. He opened his mouth to speak and then closed it.

"I'm a lot to take in. I mean, you did go to great lengths to make certain I was dead. It's a shame you didn't realize I was in the Alps."

"It can't be." Johnson finally found his voice.

"Oh, but it is. Now, here's what you need to do. I could just return to power. After all, I'm not dead." Jack let that sink in for a moment. "I could just say it was all a terrible mistake and I had no idea what had happened. My reasoning for not returning sooner was that you figured out that it wasn't me who died, but my double. So, of course, for you to remain in power I was kidnapped. And we both know that I'll be believed over you."

"What do you want?" Johnson was visibly shaken.

"Revenge!"

"What do you mean you don't make banana nut anymore?" Maheu yelled at the poor little clerk behind the glass at Baskin Robbins. "How the hell can I get some?"

"I don't know, sir," the young lady answered, "I can give you the number for headquarters."

"You'll CALL them. NOW!" Maheu bellowed. Backing away from him, she turned and picked up the phone.

Jim Angelton waited until Onassis answered the phone, "Meyer won't do it. I'll have to kill her myself."

"Well then hurry up and do it. The risks are greater every day. She's been seen with a man. If she tells him or anyone else for that matter, it'll be harder to contain."

"I'll handle it. What about Cord?"

"Leave him. He'll be dealt with later." Onassis slammed down the receiver into its cradle with a mighty crash. Anger radiated from every pore as he stormed across the room turning over a large armchair in his wake. Righting the offending chair, he blew out a sigh, and settled down to a glass of whiskey.

Johnson picked up the phone, "Jenkins, I want you to stop sending out 'advisors' to Vietnam. I need a halt on all war planes, ships, and men until further notice."

"Yes, Mr. President. I assume there is a valid reason for this untimely request."

"There is and it's none of your damned business." Johnson hung up the phone as Lancer nodded approval.

"Just remember, Lyndon, I know all about the munitions deals between you, Onassis, Jenkins, McIntyre, and Senator Smith." Jack paused for a moment to let that sink in, "And for security, I have passed this damning information along to my brothers. I know you are the one who changed the route the day of the motorcade and are responsible for my assassination, and so does J. Edgar Hoover. Despite what you have tried to do with the rigged Warren Commission report, I know. We have enough evidence from Jenkins' own military codes, ordered that day, and Roselli's own testimony to a few of my comrades that will put you in prison for life."

"I understand. The orders will stand." Johnson watched as Jack left through the French doors he'd come through. *They'll stand until I actually see you dead. Then I'll move forward.*

Chapter 31

Robert Kennedy sat in his new office in New York City. He picked up the telephone when his receptionist informed him his party was on the line. "Prince Saud, it is very good of you to take this time to visit with me."

"My pleasure, Mr. Kennedy, what can I do for you today?"

"I was hoping we could make good on a favor Saudi Arabia owes the United States. I'm sure you recall my brother sent our warplanes to help you defeat the attack by Egypt."

"Indeed I do. A very great favor was bestowed upon us by the generosity of John F Kennedy and your country."

"This favor is very simple and won't actually cost you anything. I want you to find some reason to turn Onassis down on the oil deal he wants with Saudi Arabia." Bobby leaned back in his leather chair and breathed a sigh of relief as the prince agreed. "Thank you so much. When will you gain the throne?"

"In December."

"Congratulations. I look forward to doing what I can to help you in the future, King Saud." Bobby deliberately called him by the new title as a show of respect.

Prince Rainier was handed the telegram:

I understand the negotiations with Onassis aren't going well. STOP I'm willing to buy out his shares. STOP Name your price. STOP Joseph Kennedy STOP

The prince laid the telegram down on the desk, leaned back, and lit a cigarette. He thought about it for a moment and then pressed the call button on his phone system. When the trusted assistant opened the door, he leaned forward in his chair.

"I need a telegram sent."

"Yes, your grace."

"Take this down and send it immediately.

I will accept your offer. STOP. I request nine and a half million dollars, American. STOP. Once the money has been received I will break my allegiance with Onassis. STOP. Gratefully, Prince Rainier of Monaco. STOP"

Jack Lancer opened the paper to read with his coffee.

"Breaking News – Howard Hughes has apparently landed in Las Vegas and is now in residence at the Desert Inn. His business manager has stated that there will be two hundred gallons of Banana Nut ice cream from Baskin Robbins shipped to the resort for Mr. Hughes' indulgences."

Jack finished the article and laughed out loud. He picked up the telephone and called Bobby, "Hey Bob, did you see this article about Howard Hughes?"

"Yes, that's a lot of ice cream."

"But did you send someone to rescue him? Who is his business manager?" Jack asked.

"I didn't send anyone. Because I resigned my post as Attorney General, I pushed that over to Stansel to deal with."

"I'll check with him. I wonder if Hughes is still under the control of the Mormon Mafia." Jack smiled as the door opened and Mary came into the room wearing nothing but the necklace he'd just given her. "I have to go, Bob. I'll check with you later."

He hung up the receiver and watched as she seductively glided over to him. He kissed her smooth skin. "Does this mean you're willing to go live in a safe house with me?"

She laughed, a sexy, throaty sound, "Not yet, lover, but I might still be persuaded."

Thomas McIntyre closed the door behind Jim Angelton. He breathed a sigh of relief that the man had finally left his office. Onassis had insisted on bigger docks and more space in the shipping lanes for his 'Turkish Cigarettes'.

"Robert Kennedy is on the telephone for you." The voice buzzed over the intercom.

"McIntyre. What can I do for you, Senator Kennedy?"

"That's flattering, but a little premature." Bobby laughed.

"We all know you'll win by a landslide, especially if your dad has anything to say about it."

Bobby ignored the insult. "I have business with you, McIntyre. I've heard rumors that the deal with Onassis is getting a bit trickier than you'd like to deal with. I've heard he can be pushy and shrewd in getting what he wants. I'd like to offer you a way out."

"Really? What do you possibly have to offer me?" McIntyre snorted.

"Don't be rude or I won't help you out of this jam."

"Okay, let's hear it." McIntyre conceded.

"Yes, we know I'll win the senate vote. I also have lots of sway here in the Eastern region. What if I promised you that your state would be the first one to have a state lottery? That would provide enough revenue for the deal with Onassis to simply slide by the wayside or sink like one of his barnacle ridden ships."

"It's something to think about." McIntyre thought about it. "If you can make that promise, then it's a deal."

Johnson sat on a park bench near the Potomac River. Onassis stood on the shore near him. "I've lost the deals with Saudi and Monaco. Do you have any idea why?" Onassis stormed closer to the President. Jenkins stood on duty a few feet away and watched Onassis with weariness.

"Yes, that bastard Kennedy is behind it all. He wants revenge on us." Johnson sneered the words, "He's trying to blackmail me into keeping the troops here instead of escalating this into a war as we had decided."

"What does Kennedy have over you that has stalled everything?" Onassis sat down on the bench beside Johnson.

"He's alive, that's what. He knows everything. He's told his brother and J. Edgar Hoover everything. I don't know what else to do except lay low."

"How the hell does Robert Kennedy know so much?" Onassis screamed scaring the birds into flight.

"Robert? Oh, not Robert. John."

Prince Rainier stood at the head of the table. His board of directors were all assembled, "I've received the money from America. I won't say who it came from but I have been able to reacquire the Societe de Baies de Mer. We have full control over our company once again without the encumbrances of Onassis."

"We're saved!" The men slapped one another on the back and celebrated with wine.

Jack watched as Stansel entered the little diner. "I want to thank you for meeting me like this. I have two questions. One: who is the business manager for Howard Hughes?"

Stansel looked through his notes, "I believe it was announced yesterday that Robert Maheu will be the business manager for Hughes and all inquiries will be directed to him."

"So, he's still under Onassis' control." Jack sighed.

"Yes, but at least he's here and not on that island. People at least know that he's alive."

"It's not enough."

"Look, Jack, what can you do about it?" Stansel pointed at the coffee pot the waitress had in her hand. She brought cups and poured for them.

"Thank you, that'll be all for now." Jack smiled up at the cute brunette.

"Actually, I'd like some apple pie." Stansel winked at her. She turned red and scurried off.

"Question two: when can you get us to the safe house? Mary has finally agreed that she'll go."

"I'll have to find that one out. It shouldn't be more than a couple of weeks at the longest. I also need to tell you that Smith and Wesson are being pulled from guarding her. There won't be a replacement sent." The waitress put the warm apple pie in front of him. He smiled and winked again. "I may want her number."

"You're a dirty old man. Leave her alone. She's young enough to be your daughter." Jack fumed, "What do you want me to tell Mary to do? We all know the CIA is after her."

"Stay with her. Don't let her out of your sight and we'll get you moved to a safer place in the next few hours. Where can I find you later today?"

"We'll be at O'Donnell's."

"I'll call you or have a plan by five." Stansel finished his pie in record time. "You don't mind getting the check? I've got to run."

Jack sat there bewildered for several moments before he paid the check, left a generous tip, and went to tell Mary the so-so news.

Chapter 32

"But Lee, I just don't understand why they all hate me." Jackie was near tears as she sat next to her sister on the sofa.

"Who is 'they all'?" Lee asked.

"I picked up the paper today and read this story about this absolutely horrible woman – and it was me! I just don't understand sometimes why they work so hard at hurting me. There are so many important things to do. Why pick on me?" Jackie wiped away a tear.

"Perhaps, it's because Aristotle Onassis is always here. It's like once you moved to New York you threw caution to the wind. Now, your reputation is in the trash. Everyone knows why he comes here. Most of us are adults and understand basic anatomy. You should try to control yourself a little more. You have no decorum." Lee smiled to lessen the impact of her brutal honesty.

"You don't know what it's like. Jack would take me back in a heartbeat if I'd have him, but I won't, I can't. What kind of life would that be?"

"I've lost you again, haven't I?" Lee watched as Jackie wiped her non-existent tear from her eye.

245

"No, he's alive. Bobby knows it. I'm sure that Ethel and Pat know too. Why doesn't he just give the game up and announce to everyone he was lost or something. I want to go back to being the President's First Lady. I don't like everyone being so rude and hateful to me." Jackie shed a few real tears as Lee leaned over to pat her shoulder.

"Look honey, I really believe you need to check yourself in somewhere. This delusion is getting worse." Lee watched her closer.

"He came to see me, you know, at Ari's party in the Hamptons. He was dressed as a waiter and he found me in the garden. I was horrible to him. Maybe I am getting what I deserve."

"Did anyone else see him there, Jacks?"

"No, he said no one could see him or it would mess everything up." Jackie shook her head. "I told him I tell the kids about him every night because it makes the Camelot dream seem real."

"What a perfectly horrid thing to say to anyone. I can understand why people attack you." Lee stood up. "I'll give you some advice. Don't marry Aristotle Onassis. If you think people hate you now, they really will if you end up with that lousy son of a bitch."

Jack and Mary waited by the telephone at Kenny O'Donnell's house. It was nearly five o'clock when the phone rang. They both nearly jumped out of their skin. "Hello?" Jack answered before the first ring ended.

Stansel asked, "Ready to move?"

"Yes, we're ready."

"Okay, Latimer will pick you up in ten minutes and take you to one of the safe locations here in D.C. for now. Then we'll find a permanent place for you. Hopefully, you can go stay where the others are. Sorry for being cryptic, but I'm sure you understand." Stansel hung up before Jack could say any more.

"He's not dead?" Ari looked at Johnson.

"No."

"Then he must die. Everything depends on it. I'll take care of it myself." Onassis got up and left Johnson sitting there, hoping that the Greek bastard really could take care of it.

The quartet rode along the city streets of Wishbone while Maf hung his head out of the car window. They were just driving around getting to know their new surroundings. Norma suddenly grabbed Bill's arm, "Stop! Oh please stop. There, just over there." Bill pulled up to a closed store front on Main Street.

"What is it?" Bill asked as he put the car in park.

"I want to go look at it." Norma opened her car door and jumped out still clutching Maf. "It's perfect. The location, the size, well just everything." Norma had pressed her nose against the glass and strained to see the interior.

Bill watched her for a moment before he dared to ask her, "Perfect for what?"

"My acting studio. I've dreamed of one for so long but now, now I've actually seen it. Let's see if we can get inside." Norma tried the door but it was securely locked.

"I'll have to make an appointment." Bill jotted down the number written in large black letters on a piece of paper taped to the inside of the door.

Norma looked around, there was a little boutique next door. "I'll be right back. Barbara do you want to come?"

The Morris' had gotten out of the car when Bill did and they all stood watching Norma.

"Sure thing." Barbara caught up to Norma. "I hope they know something."

"Maybe they've got a key and we can get in." Norma pushed the door open and the brass bell above the door tinkled their arrival as they walked into the quaint little shop.

The clerk came from the back, "How can I help you?"

"Do you know who owns the empty space next door?" Norma asked as she pointed to the right.

"Sure I do. I'm the owner. I'm Gladys Wimberly and who might this be?" she scratched the dog under his chin. "What is your interest?"

"Hi Mrs. Wimberly, I'm Norma Walton, this little fluff ball is Maf, and this is my dear friend, Barbara Morris. I'd like to see if the space would work for a studio."

Mrs. Wimberly smiled, "Of course it would. Hang on, I'll get the key." She went around behind the counter and came back with a set of keys. "Come on over, I'll give you the grand tour."

October 12, 1964

Ethel answered the door, to her surprise it was Rose. "Rose, come in."

Ethel led her mother-in-law into the den and helped her take a seat. "Can I get you something?"

"No, dear, I'll only be a moment. I have a horrible feeling that something is going to happen to one of the boys. I think it might be John."

"Rose, you know he's already gone." Ethel tried to soothe her.

"No, no he isn't. He's going to be soon though. I feel it in my blood. I lost him, only to briefly find him and now I'm never going to see him alive again. Please, Ethel. You must help me. If you know where he is, you must warn him." Rose stood up and paced, too agitated to sit still.

"Rose, he's gone." Ethel tried to speak in a calming tone.

"Not yet, but he will be. Where is Bobby? New York?"

"Yes, he spends most of his time there now." Ethel agreed, "Do you want me to call him?"

"Only if he knows where John is right now, otherwise it's no use." Rose broke into tears. "I really thought you would help me."

"I can't help you. I'm so sorry, Rose." Ethel too began to cry, and the women held on to each other as though the assassination had just happened this instant.

Mary and Jack walked hand-in-hand in Georgetown. They had wandered around all afternoon taking in the fresh crisp air of the autumn day and dreading tomorrow.

"Stansel will be livid when he finds we've escaped for the day." Jack turned to Mary and kissed her lips softly, "It'll be worth his wrath to give you just one more day of freedom."

Mary hugged him close. "Is this house going to be nice?"

Jack smiled down on her, "Yes, it has a lake around it and there are lots of open spaces but mostly it'll be quiet. We'll have to get used to playing checkers or cards with Georgi and Marita. I hope they've become friends."

"No politics? No Castro wanting to blow up the world? No Khrushchev trying to escape being overthrown? What will we talk about?" Mary asked with a tear in her eye.

"The children we're going to have?" Jack led her toward the Old Chesapeake and Ohio Canal tow path. It was wooded, private, and secluded for a little afternoon love making.

She breathed in deep as they rounded the corner and the Potomac River came into full view. "I love it here. Just in this very spot. Please can we stop for a while and watch the river?"

Jack took off his jacket and laid it on the ground for her to sit on. He snuggled in close to her as they watched the boats slowly glide by, silent and beautiful. The peace was perfect. She sighed into his arms as she leaned closer to him.

"It won't be so bad, you know. I'm sure you can paint and do what you love. Maybe you could even get someone to take your paintings into the town flea market and sell them for you." Jack kissed the tip of her nose.

"Maybe. I hope we won't regret doing this." Mary looked into his eyes.

"If we don't do this we'll be dead in a few days. Thankfully, no one knows we're here or we could be sitting ducks right now."

They glanced around nervously and laughed. "I don't need this right now. I'm spooked enough as it is. Let's go back." Mary suddenly got up.

Before Jack could stand to his feet two shots rang out, shattering the still day.

"Someone help me. Someone help. . .." two more shots rang out and Mary fell headlong into the grass. The blood oozing from her head and neck. She starred open eyed into the nothingness of death.

Jack crawled to her, screaming her name over and over again. He held her lifeless body in his strong arms and then tried to pick her up.

A kick leveled him on the ground. He looked up into the cold, hate filled eyes of Aristotle Onassis.

"You killed her you son of a bitch. You killed her!" Jack lunged at him, grabbing him around the knees. They wrestled to the ground briefly until Onassis whacked Jack with the butt of his gun, knocking him out cold.

When Jack awoke a few moments later, Mary was gone. Onassis was leaning against a tree with a gun pointed at Jack's chest.

Stansel entered the safe house in D.C. and found it in an uproar. He dropped the pizza box on the kitchen table. He ran to find Latimer. "Where are they?"

Latimer turned from the two plain clothes agents who had scoured the entire area, "We don't know. They've vanished."

"How did this happen?"

"First Jack went to the bathroom and then Mary said she wasn't feeling well and wanted to go lie down. I didn't think anything about it for about ten minutes. But then Jack didn't come back. I went looking for him, he was gone and so was Mary. They escaped out of the window in the upstairs bathroom. I would have sworn he was too big to get out of there or I would have stayed with him."

"Latimer, stay here. You two come with me. I need every cop you can find on this right now." Stansel screamed orders as they rushed out into the darkening afternoon.

Jack looked around him. He'd been moved. The river was no longer visible nor was that horrible spot where Mary had died.

Onassis gave him a minute to come to fully, "Such a shame about your lover." Ari mocked.

Jack sat there silent.

"You know I'm going to kill you." Onassis waved the gun for emphasis.

"Yes." Jack sat up straight, "I'm sure you want to finish the job you botched the first time. Sloppy, it's not like you."

"I thought you were dead for the better part of a year. If it hadn't been for that fool Duvalier, I never would have believed you were still among the living." Onassis shook his head, "You do manage to make my life a living hell. Jackie told me numerous times you were alive, but I chose to believe she was delusional with grief."

Jack laughed out loud, a genuine hearty sound that pissed Onassis off more than he cared to let on. "Jacks? That woman has no emotion except greed. No, that's not an emotion, but she makes it seem like it should be. You're in for a rare treat and a run for your money if you do marry her. My condolences."

"You're not afraid to die are you?" Aristotle seemed bemused. "Why?"

"My life ended when the poor chap in the motorcade died. My life, as I knew it was gone. So why should I be afraid now?"

Onassis nodded and thought about it for a second. "I've finally got you in my grasp, and oh there is no doubt, I'll kill you but first you have to know the reason."

"Must I? You see, I don't really care what the reason is." Jack watched Ari for a moment and looked around the trees.

"Too damn bad. First off, you wouldn't let me have any docks in the U.S."

"Not just me. No one wants to do business with you. Have you not noticed that the Saudi's and Prince of Monaco have deserted you?"

"What do you know about that?"

"I'm the one who started those balls rolling. You're a bastard and you don't deserve to have any part of America. You have to earn respect and you haven't been able to do that."

"I've always hated you because you had Jackie." Aristotle told him.

"You can have her. She'll hurt you and disappoint you, but as long as you know that up front, you can't say you weren't warned." Jack leaned his head against the tree.

"Jack! Jack!" Stansel ran toward the Potomac River with two uniformed police officers. He spotted a figure lying on the ground. As they grew closer he could tell it was a woman. She was lying at an odd angle. There was a black man standing near her in the water. He appeared to be in shock.

Stansel motioned for the officers to take care of it as he ran deeper into the woods, "Jack! Where are you?"

Pop! Pop! Stansel followed the sound and found Jack, shot between the eyes, leaning against a tree. "Damn it! Damn it! Damn it!" He ran after whoever had shot Jack Lancer but the woods were getting dark and the figures were blurring.

He turned back to John Fitzgerald Kennedy and kicked his shoe. "You bloody fool!" He yelled at no one. "You damned bloody fool."

The End

Epilogue

Norma sat on the wrap around porch with Barbara. They were watching the men ride their horses up the drive, still some distance away.

"I can't believe how quickly they've taken to this ranching business." Norma grinned as she sipped her iced tea.

"Greg grew up on a farm in Idaho." Barbara waved at the men as they drew closer. "They need a herding dog."

The phone rang, Norma stood up as Maf jumped out of her lap. He followed her inside the house to the kitchen. Barbara heard Norma's "Oh no!" and raced into the house after her friend.

Norma held up a finger, signaling that Barbara wait a minute. "Oh Ethel, that's terrible."

Norma sat down on a kitchen chair and Maf jumped back into her lap. She stroked him absent mindedly as she listened to Ethel.

After a few minutes, she wiped a tear away, "Thanks for calling Ethel. I'm so sorry."

Barbara leaned forward and patted Norma's arm. Norma smiled and swiped at another tear, "Yes, thanks for calling. . .we'll talk again soon." Norma handed the receiver to Barbara.

The men came into the house just as Barbara sat back down next to Norma. Bill came over to kiss his bride but noticed her sadness. She looked at them, "Jack. He's dead."

"What happened?" Bill asked with gentle concern.

"He was killed in Chesapeake near the Potomac. Mary was killed as well. Stansel found John and they discreetly took him away. No one will ever know he was there. Mary was shot with a different caliber weapon. They found a suspect and are holding him but the weapon hasn't been recovered."

"Oh, honey, I'm so sorry." Bill leaned down and hugged his wife as Maf struggled to lick her face. Bill took Maf and handed him to Barbara.

"When did all of this happen?" Barbara asked as Greg took her hand. He'd been standing just inside the kitchen door listening.

"Mid-October. Ethel has just now gotten herself together enough to let us know. Of course we don't get a lot of D.C. news here so we couldn't have known about Mary either. She wasn't a celebrity or anyone who would have merited national attention." Norma tried a watery little half smile. "Well, we tried."

"Yes you did. I'm so sorry." Greg came forward and took her hand for a moment, squeezed it, and released it. Bill stood up and Maf wiggled out of Barbara's arms and found the lap of his *mama.*

"Bobby told reporters that he wanted to move his brother from Arlington Cemetery to the family plot in Hyannis Port. Of course, they didn't move the body buried in Arlington but they were able to have a small family service for John. Ethel said Rose kept saying over and over, 'I told you, Nellie, I told you.' It was a sad thing for her to have to bury him twice."

Norma stood up. "I'm okay. That's all I really know for now."

"Honey, why don't we go for a walk? I bet the Morris' won't mind taking care of dinner for tonight under the circumstances."

"Of course we will." Barbara hugged Norma, "Go for a walk, honey. Clear your head and talk it over. We'll be fine."

The Waltons left the house and circled around to a small pond about a quarter mile away. They held hands and Bill kept his silence.

"Ethel said that Mary had some friends go to the house looking for her and they found Jim Angelton there tearing up the place. They were looking for the diary. I hope they never find it." Norma kicked a rock on the path and Maf barked at her feet.

"I'm sure they won't and it'll be a small bit of justice for Mary." Bill squeezed her hand and they continued walking.

"I know we haven't really talked about it since we looked at the studio but I really want to do it. Especially now. I feel like my life will be wasted if I don't somehow give something back. I have all the money Ethel and Bobby paid me for being a nanny socked away. It'll pay for the place and the little bit of remodeling I'll need to do. I'd only do it part time and when I have students. I'll place an advertisement in the newspaper and get clients that way at first. I'd like to eventually put on one act plays for the town, when I feel the students are good enough." Norma took a deep breath and turned to Bill. "What do you think?"

"I think, you're an incredibly amazing woman and you'll make an excellent instructor." Bill hugged her close. "We'll call Mrs. Wimberly when we get back to the house and tell her."

She bounced up and down on the balls of her feet and did a small pirouette. "Oh, thank you!"

He laughed as she took off running back to the house, "I have to tell Barbara!" Maf ran behind her, little legs flying across the dirt and barking merrily all the way home.

From the Authors

We had a lot of fun creating this alternate history of not only Marilyn Monroe, but also of John F Kennedy. We hope you enjoyed reading it.

Look for exciting new titles as we continue to bring light and life to infamous people in history.

The prelude to the What She Knew trilogy will be out soon.

We would love to hear from you! To post a review, simply go to our Amazon book page. If you would like to stay in touch with us, you can go to the following link and sign up for our newsletter.

www.whatsheknew.wixsite.com/kandtproductions.com

Authors Page

K. R. Hughes is a native of Amarillo, TX. She has a degree in English, helps with literacy programs and tutors' college students. Hughes has two children, Justin and Kayti. Hughes also has two regency, historical novels, "Treasured Love" and "Lord Tristan's True Love," under her pen name Kymber Lee.

T. L. Burns is the foremost researcher and historical guru for the What She Knew Trilogy. Burns and husband Ken have two grown children, Kenny and Deven. Burns is a native of California. She has spent the majority of her adult life working with at-risk kids and adults.

Both authors currently reside in Las Vegas, NV where they write and encourage budding authors to follow their dreams. You can connect with them at any of the following social media groups:

www.facebook.com/HughesBurns

www.twitter.com/whatsheknewbook

www.whatsheknew.wix.com/kandtproductions

Cast of Historical Characters

Norma Baker (a.k.a. Marilyn Monroe)– sex goddess and movie star in the 1950's and 1960's.

Barbara Hadley – Norma's best friend and confidante.

John F Kennedy – president of the United States, nickname Jack. Married to **Jacqueline Bouvier Kennedy**.

Robert F Kennedy – brother to John F Kennedy and Attorney General for the United States, nickname Bobby. Married to **Ethel Kennedy**.

Patricia Lawford Kennedy – sister to John and Robert Kennedy and married to **Peter Lawford,** movie star, one of the Rat Pack.

Joe Kennedy - father of John, Bobby, and Patricia; married to **Rose Kennedy**.

Lee Radizwill - **Jacqueline Kennedy's** sister; married to **Prince Stasnislaw Radizwill** (aka Stas).

Teddy Kennedy - younger brother of John and Bobby.

Kenny O'Donnell - was an American political consultant who served as the special assistant and appointments secretary to U.S. President **John F. Kennedy**

Frank Sinatra – crooner, movie star and Rat Pack leader, political ally to John F. Kennedy.

Lee Harvey Oswald - was an American sniper who assassinated President John F. Kennedy on November 22, 1963.

Bill Walton – was the CIA operative who was the liaison to the Soviet Union.

Sam Giancana – mobster who wanted to further his career with anyone who paid well, also associated with Frank Sinatra and Jimmy Hoffa.

Fidel Castro – Dictator over Cuba, who had an alliance with Russia.

Nikita Sergeyevich Khrushchev - was a politician who led the Soviet Union during part of the Cold War. He served as First Secretary of the Communist Party of the Soviet Union from 1953 to 1964

Aristotle Onassis – Greek business tycoon. Bobby Kennedy was his arch enemy. He provided major business deals in the US through his shipping business – illegally.

François Duvalier, also known as **Papa Doc**, was the President of Haiti from 1957 to 1971

Mary Meyer – Her ex-husband is **Cord Meyer**. He works for the CIA in the 'dirty tricks' dept. She's a long-time lover of John F Kennedy.

Lyndon B. Johnson - Vice President to John F. Kennedy and became the 36th president of the U.S. when Kennedy was assassinated. He is married to **Lady Bird Johnson**.

Madeliene Brown - was an American woman who stated that she was a longtime mistress of U.S. President Lyndon B. Johnson.

Walter Wilson Jenkins - was an American political figure and longtime top aide to U.S. President Lyndon B. Johnson.

J. Edgar Hoover - the first Director of the Federal Bureau of Investigation (FBI) of the United States. Appointed director of the Bureau of Investigation— predecessor to the FBI in 1924.

Howard Hughes - an American business magnate, aviator, aerospace engineer, film maker and philanthropist. He was one of the wealthiest people in the world, and very eccentric.

Senator Margaret Chase Smith – A member of the Republican Party, she served as a U.S. Senator (1949-1973) from Maine. A moderate Republican, she is perhaps best remembered for her 1950 speech, "Declaration of Conscience," in which she criticized the tactics of McCarthyism.

Smith was an unsuccessful candidate for the Republican nomination in the 1964 presidential election, but was the first woman to be placed in nomination for the presidency at a major party's convention.